**The Cattaneos' Christmas Miracles**
*A family reunited for a Christmas to remember!*

*A life-changing letter*

Millionaire Leo Baxter is shocked to receive a letter
from his biological parents, but tragedy strikes
before they get the chance to meet. Now he has
two siblings who want to see him...

*A long-lost brother*

Sebastian and Noemi Cattaneo are in the
Swiss Alps for their parents' will reading. With a
multimillion-euro business at stake and a surprise
in store, it looks set to be...

*A Christmas to remember!*

Can the most magical time of the year—and finding
love along the way—give this family the miracles
they've each been waiting for?

Find out in

*Cinderella's New York Christmas* by Scarlet Wilson
Available now!

*Heiress's Royal Baby Bombshell* by Jennifer Faye
Coming November 2018!

*CEO's Marriage Miracle* by Sophie Pembroke
Coming December 2018!

Dear Reader,

Christmas is my favorite time of year, and there was something so magical about getting to write a story for this time of year with elements of *Cinderella* attached to it.

I've been lucky enough to visit New York when it's blanketed with snow (our plane almost didn't land!) so I've seen lots of the sights that are described here. Looking out from the Top of the Rock was one of my favorites, along with seeing Central Park completely covered in snow, and seeing the dinosaurs and blue whale in the American Museum of Natural History.

It's a horrible time of year to be lonely and, essentially, that's what's wrong with my two characters, Leo and Anissa. Finding each other and connecting at Christmastime seems to weave a spell around them and helps them realize what is most important. Here's hoping you enjoy this story as much as I enjoyed writing it.

I love to hear from readers—feel free to contact me via my website, scarlet-wilson.com.

Lots of love,

*Scarlet Wilson*

# *Cinderella's New York Christmas*

*Scarlet Wilson*

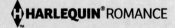

**HARLEQUIN** ROMANCE

Recycling programs for this product may not exist in your area.

Special thanks and acknowledgment are given to Scarlet Wilson for her contribution to The Cattaneos' Christmas Miracles series.

ISBN-13: 978-1-335-13531-5

Cinderella's New York Christmas

First North American publication 2018

Copyright © 2018 by Harlequin Books S.A.

Printed in U.S.A.

**Scarlet Wilson** writes for both Harlequin Romance and Medical Romance. She lives on the west coast of Scotland with her fiancé and their two sons. She loves to hear from readers and can be reached via her website, scarlet-wilson.com.

## Books by Scarlet Wilson

## Harlequin Romance

*The Italian Billionaire's New Year Bride*

### Summer at Villa Rosa

*The Mysterious Italian Houseguest*

### Maids Under the Mistletoe

*Christmas in the Boss's Castle*

### Tycoons in a Million

*Holiday with the Millionaire*
*A Baby to Save Their Marriage*

### The Vineyards of Calanetti

*His Lost-and-Found Bride*

## Harlequin Medical Romance

*One Kiss in Tokyo...*
*A Royal Baby for Christmas*
*The Doctor and the Princess*
*A Family Made at Christmas*
*Resisting the Single Dad*
*Locked Down with the Army Doc*

Visit the Author Profile page at Harlequin.com for more titles.

To my fab NHS work colleagues Kathleen Winter
and Janice Traynor. I value the fact I work with
such kind, supportive friends.

## Praise for
## Scarlet Wilson

"Charming, compelling and absolutely impossible
to put down, *Christmas in the Boss's Castle* is
another outstanding romance from the wonderfully
talented Scarlet Wilson!"

*—Goodreads*

# PROLOGUE

*Our dearest Leo,*

*You have no idea how much joy it gives us to write this letter. We have hoped and prayed for this moment for so long. We hope you are well, we hope you are healthy, and we want you to know that we've spent every day thinking about you, and the last thirty-five years looking for you. You have always been in our hearts, Leo, always. Please believe that.*

*Thirty-eight years ago we were young, foolish teenagers who fell in love. Our parents disapproved and when we fell pregnant with you we were forced to give you up for adoption.*

*We want you to know that it was never what we wanted. From the very first moment we knew you existed we wanted to keep you. But times were different then. Our parents bullied us, refused to sup-*

port our relationship, and were ashamed of their illegitimate grandchild.

It broke our hearts, but we were penniless and had to agree to give you up for adoption, or we would have both been flung out of our homes.

Every day we talked about you and imagined where you were. We prayed you had parents who loved you as much as we did, and who nurtured and supported you.

Despite what our families thought, we stayed together and eventually married. As soon as we had some money we started our search for you. But the world was full of paper records then—people who kept secrets and those who told lies. It took years for us to learn you'd gone to the US, and then the trail went dead.

It broke our hearts all over again.

You have a brother, Sebastian, and a sister, Noemi. We always found it difficult to talk about your adoption to your siblings, but now that we've found you we would love it if our family could be reunited.

It has always been our dream that one day we could have all our children sitting around our table for Christmas dinner, like the true family we always wanted *to be. We would love it if this could come true this year and wish that you could join us at Mont Coeur, Switzerland—the place where we have always loved to spend Christmas.*

*We've missed you every day, Leo.*

*Knowing that you are alive and well has brought us so much joy. We know you may be settled in your life. We know that you may well think of your adoptive parents as your only parents, and we will always respect your decisions and your wishes, but, please, please consider our request to meet.*

*There is nothing we want more than to throw our arms around our firstborn son and tell you how much we love you.*
*With our hearts,*
*Mamma e Papà*
*Salvo and Nicole Cattaneo*

# CHAPTER ONE

HE SHOULD NEVER have opened that letter.

His insides curled uncomfortably as he took the final few steps up to the veranda around the luxury chalet. Even though it was the beginning of November it seemed the Mont Coeur ski resort in Switzerland had moved into full Christmas mode. Maybe it was the cold weather and snow that made the whole population think it was normal to have Christmas trees up at the beginning of November. But as his car had woven its way through the resort it had seemed that every business and shop in Mont Coeur was fully on board for the festive season.

Everywhere he looked there were garlands, twinkling lights and piped music.

On any other day he'd think the whole place was picture perfect—like a scene on one of those Christmas cards. But today wasn't like any other day.

His parents' luxury chalet seemed to be a

leader in the festive decorations. Through the glass-panelled doors he could see the Christmas tree decorated in reds and gold as a focal point in the spacious living area; boughs of holly had been wound around the banisters and across the mantelpiece, where a fire was roaring beneath. And above him, against night sky, gold twinkling fairy lights adorned the outside of the chalet. The quintessential idyllic Christmas scene.

This should be different. This should be so different.

He should be coming here today to meet the parents who had given him up for adoption thirty-eight years ago. He should be coming here to learn more about the people who'd said they'd thought about him every day since. Instead, he was here at the insistence of a family lawyer he didn't know and a sister, Noemi, whom he'd never met, for the reading of his parents' will.

The warmth and the family feel of the chalet felt totally alien to him. He'd never experienced this lifestyle. He'd never experienced the true joy of a happy, family Christmas. And he couldn't shake the guilty feeling that if he hadn't been found, hadn't answered their letter, then his parents would never have died in a helicopter crash on their way to meet him.

Now he was here at their request for the will reading—and to meet his two siblings.

Everything about this felt awkward and wrong.

His stomach churned again as he knocked on the glass door. Maybe no one was home? Maybe his siblings had changed their minds? It would be so much easier to turn on his heel, go back and find the alternative luxury chalet his PA had booked for him.

There was a flicker behind the glass. A woman rushed towards him. She was tall and slim with a short brown angled bob. Behind her, walking much more warily, was a tall, muscular man. Even from here Leo could see the creases along his brow.

The woman flung the door open. 'Leo?'

Her brown eyes were hopeful. He could see her hands twitching at her sides. She was barely able to contain herself.

'Yes,' he replied hoarsely. It was all it took.

She let out a squeal and flung her arms around his neck. 'Oh, Leo, I'm so glad to finally meet you.'

He stood frozen to the spot, not sure of whether he should lift his arms to hug this woman back. After what seemed like the longest time she finally pulled back, wiping a tear from her eye. 'I'm Noemi. You know that, don't you?' She wiped away another tear and gestured to the man behind her. 'And this is Sebastian, your brother.'

It had to be the most awkward meeting in history. Animosity was rolling off Sebastian in waves. He didn't even step forward, just gave the barest nod of his head.

Leo steadied himself for a second. This was his brother and sister. When he'd been growing up he'd always wished he was part of a large family. He would have loved to have had a brother and sister. But his adoptive parents had already decided one child was too much. He was never quite sure why they'd adopted him as they'd shown so little interest in him.

All he wanted to do right now was turn and walk out the door. It made him feel pathetic. He was a businessman, a CEO. He spent his life in difficult business dealings. This should be nothing to him. But everything about this was unravelling a whole pile of emotions that he'd never acknowledged.

It was obvious that everyone in Mont Coeur was rich, even by his standards, his brother and sister included. Maybe they were worried he was here for money? Money that he didn't need or want.

Noemi grabbed his hand. 'Come in, Leo, come in. I want to hear all about you. I want to know how you are.' She bit her bottom lip as a few more tears escaped. Was his sister always this tearful? He wasn't big on emotion at the best of times and he was already feeling the overload.

Her hands were warm against his chilly skin and she pulled him inside. She drew him straight into the heart of the house, between the Christmas tree and the fireplace. 'Give me your jacket,' she said enthusiastically, tugging his dark wool coat from his shoulders.

Sebastian had barely moved. The muscles around the bottom of his neck were tense. He glanced at Leo as he shrugged his way out of his coat. His words were stiff. 'My wife, Maria, and son, Frankie, hoped to be here but...' his voice tailed as if he were trying to decide what to say '...they've been unavoidably delayed.'

Something in his gut told Leo that Sebastian hadn't been exactly truthful when he'd spoken. He looked like a coil about to burst from into a spring. Either his wife and son didn't want to meet the 'new' brother, or Sebastian was hiding something else completely. Leo had done enough business dealings to know when someone was being economical with the truth.

Noemi patted the sofa next to her. 'Please, sit. Giovanni will be here soon, but I want a chance to chat first.'

Giovanni. The family lawyer who'd persuaded him to attend the reading of the will.
Giovanni, who right now he wanted to email
and tell him that he'd changed his mind.

He sat down on the sofa and was almost
swallowed up by it. Leo wanted to laugh out
loud, because that's how he was feeling in gen-
eral about the visit here.

His eyes caught sight of family pictures on
the wall. There was a whole array, obviously
taken over years, starting with a young smiling
couple with a baby and toddler, going up to four
adults all standing with their arms around each
other. Love was plainly visible in every picture.

Something gripped in his chest. The family
that he should have had. The family he should
have been part of.

It was like a million little caterpillars creep-
ing up his spine. He actually thought he might
be sick.

He wanted to go over and grab the photos,
hold them up to his nose and study his parents.
He wanted to see the last thirty-eight years.
What they'd been like, how they'd grown, how
they'd aged. All things he'd been cheated out of.

He pushed himself up from the impossible
sofa. 'This was a mistake…'

'What? No.' Noemi looked instantly stricken.
Something twisted in his chest. He really

couldn't handle this. He wasn't equipped to deal with this. He'd spent a lifetime devoid of any love. Forming relationships wasn't his forte. The last woman he'd dated had described him as 'cold' and 'hard'—two things he couldn't really deny.

Getting that initial letter from his parents had been like a bolt out of the blue. It had taken him two weeks to reply. When he had, he'd been hit by the overload that was his mother, who'd emailed every day, making plans to visit.

Getting the call from Noemi—the sister he'd never met—to tell him that their parents had been killed in a helicopter crash while on their way to visit him in New York had almost taken the air from his lungs.

He *so* wasn't ready for any of the emotions attached to having a family. Guilt. Expectation. Judgement.

He'd wanted to see them. Curiosity had made him fly to Switzerland to stand in the same room as his brother and sister and talk to them in the flesh. But now he'd done it.

He had to get out of here. He had to get some air.

A hand came down firmly on his arm. 'Don't go.'

Sebastian. His brother.

He could see Sebastian was struggling with

this too. 'Not yet.' It was almost like he couldn't quite get the words out.

Sebastian shook his head. 'You just got here.' He wasn't really meeting Leo's gaze. 'Take a breath. Take a moment.'

Leo looked to his left. Noemi's chin was trembling. He couldn't watch her cry again.

Leo couldn't work out if Sebastian was doing this for him or for his sister. Their sister. Noemi was *their* sister. Not just Sebastian's.

Brain overload. This wasn't him. Nothing about this was him. All of his life he'd been cool, calm and collected. Those three words were synonymous with how most of his work colleagues described him.

He pulled his arm away from Sebastian's. He turned to face him. 'I know I was asked to listen to the reading of the will. But now I'm here, I can see this isn't appropriate. I don't want anything from you both. I don't need anything. I'm not here to take what you think is actually yours.'

A flicker of anger flashed across Sebastian's eyes. But before he had a chance to respond there was another voice.

'Ah, Leo, I see you made it. Perfect timing.'

Leo turned to face the figure standing at the now open door. 'Giovanni Paliotta,' said the grey-haired, designer-suited man as he closed the door behind him and walked over with his hand outstretched. He tilted his head to the side as he got closer. 'It's a pleasure to meet you. You're so like your father.'

It was like a kick in the guts.

Giovanni didn't seem to notice, and waved his hand towards a large table in the corner of the room. 'Shall we sit?'

Noemi looked at the table, then glanced around the rest of the room, as if she were trying to find another place to sit, but Sebastian moved behind her, putting his arm at her waist and leading her over.

Leo's gaze flickered. Twelve chairs. Enough for a large family gathering. Was this the table that his mother and father had traditionally sat around at Christmastime? Was this the table that his mother and father had intended for him to sit around with his brother and sister?

Leo had never wanted to bolt from a place so much in his life. He steadied his breathing.

Giovanni settled in one of the chairs and spread his papers in front of him.

Sebastian and Noemi sat down with only a glance at each other. Leo took a few seconds then dragged out one of the heavy chairs too.

Giovanni waited until everyone was settled then gave them all a nod.

'We all know why we are here.' He nodded

again in particular to Leo. 'I was your parents' lawyer for the last thirty years, and I loved them, and miss them, and everything I do today is in accordance with their wishes.'

There was an edge of anxiety in Giovanni's voice that Leo picked up on. He cast his eyes over his brother and sister again as he shifted in his seat.

Giovanni started reading from the paper in front of him. 'This is the last will and testament of Salvo and Nicole Cattaneo. Salvo and Nicole were the sole owners of Cattaneo Jewels, currently valued at around seventy billion euros.'

Leo blinked. He knew the jewellery line was famous and international, but he hadn't realised his parents' fortune rivalled even his own.

Giovanni kept talking, 'It was the wish of Salvo and Nicole that in the event of their death, the business should remain with the family.' Giovanni pressed his lips together for a second, looking decidedly nervous. 'As such, the controlling stake in Cattaneo Jewels will pass to Leo Baxter, their eldest biological child.'

'What?' Sebastian's chair landed on the floor as he stood up and thumped his hands on the table.

Noemi's mouth opened, then closed again.

Giovanni cleared his throat, refusing to fix on Sebastian's red face.

'No,' said Leo, shaking his head. 'I have no interest in the family business. I don't even know anything about jewels.' He stood up too. All he wanted was to get out of there.

'I've trained for this my whole life,' raged Sebastian. 'Who is he to inherit the business over me?'

'Your brother,' snapped Giovanni. For the briefest second Leo realised why Salvo and Nicole had worked with this lawyer for thirty years.

Giovanni held up his hands. 'Sit down, both of you.'

Leo met his brother's angry gaze. He got it. He did. And he had absolutely no interest in this business, but his brother's reaction annoyed him. It didn't matter that he partially understood it. He couldn't hide his flare of anger. Sebastian had got to spend a lifetime with his parents—Leo hadn't even got to meet them.

Giovanni gave a shake of his head and Leo settled back into his chair, staring pointedly at Sebastian until he did the same.

Giovanni continued slowly. 'There are conditions attached.'

'What conditions?' Leo couldn't help it. He'd been in business too long to get caught out.

'Leo must hold the controlling stake in the business for a minimum of six months. The shares can't be sold, or transferred, to any alternative controlling company or family member.'

'What happens if he does?' Noemi's voice was shaky.

Giovanni looked at all three of them. 'Any attempt to violate the terms of the will mean that the company shall cease trading and will be liquidated with its assets distributed amongst the other existing four hundred shareholders.'

'What?' Sebastian's voice sounded wheezy. His eyes were wide.

Leo sat frozen in his chair. He was a businessman. He had a head for business. He knew exactly what this was.

'This is blackmail,' he said coldly.

'No,' said Noemi quietly.

'Manipulation, then.'

She turned to face him and gave a slow nod. 'You could be right.'

'But why?' Leo leaned across the table towards Giovanni. 'Why on earth would—' he couldn't even bring himself to say the words 'parents'—'Salvo and Nicole do this?'

Giovanni sighed and leaned back in his chair.

'Did this just happen?' interjected Sebastian angrily. 'Did they just do this because they found Leo?'

Leo drummed his fingers on the table. He

couldn't get his head around this at all. 'Were they sick?'

Giovanni started.

Leo's brain was struggling to make any sense of this at all. He asked again, 'Were they sick?' He shook his head. 'This doesn't make any sense. I don't imagine for a second that they could have predicted the accident they were in, so the only other thing I can think of was that they were sick. They were trying to find a way that we...' he paused for a second at that word '...would all have to work together. Nothing else makes sense.'

Sebastian looked pale. His eyes found Noemi. 'We would have known. They would have told us.'

She gave a bewildered shrug. 'They didn't tell us about Leo until a month ago. And only then because I found his letter.'

Giovanni cleared his throat. 'Their will has always said this.'

'What?' This time it was three voices in unison.

Giovanni gave a slow shake of his head. 'They always believed they would find Leo. Initially, the will just named him as "the eldest biological child". They never stopped searching. Even if they died before they found him, they still wanted him to know he was always part of the family, and to give him the opportunity to know the family business.' Giovanni took a deep breath. 'They believed in family. You know that.' He shook his head. 'They changed the will to include his name as soon as they found him. But the truth is he was always included. In their eyes, he was always part of the family—whether they knew his new name or not.'

Noemi blinked and looked between Leo and Sebastian. 'This isn't about the business,' she said quietly.

Leo could tell Sebastian was still angry. There was a tiny tic in his jaw. But he met his sister's gaze and gave her the slightest nod. 'I know that.' It was the most conciliatory thing he'd said since Leo had got there.

Leo felt blindsided and he hated that. Every business meeting, every potential deal, he always went in prepared. He would know the background, the finances, the personalities and their quirks before he even set foot in the room.

But here? For the first time since he'd been a child he felt totally out of his depth.

It felt as if the room was closing in around him, suffocating him with the heat from the fire, the love from the pictures on the wall, and that horrible feeling of emptiness inside.

Sebastian's voice was tight. 'Mamma and

Papà spent their lives growing this family business. It's gone from a few tiny shops in Italy to a billion-euro company with worldwide acclaim. You might know business, Leo, but you don't know *this* business. And I'm damned if I'm going to let their pride and joy fall apart around you for the next six months because you don't know what you're doing.'

He'd had enough. Leo had reached breaking point. He pulled back every emotion that he'd been struggling to keep in check. Business. Sebastian was talking business to him and no one was better at business than him.

'I might not know anything about the jewellery business, Sebastian, but one business is the same as another. Don't make any mistake, I don't want to do this, and I'm not interested in doing this. I don't need your *mamma* and *papà*'s business, and I certainly don't need their money. I could walk away right now quite happily, but where would that leave you?'

He let the words hang in the air. Noemi's face was pale as she stood up and reached out and took Leo's hand, stumbling. Leo caught her elbow but Sebastian was at her side in an instant. 'Are you okay?' He slid his arm around her waist, helping to prop her up. It was like she was caught between two brothers.

She gave a shake of her head as she steadied herself for a few seconds, one hand still holding Leo's. 'Just a bit dizzy.' She pressed her other hand against her stomach as she took some slow breaths and the colour in her cheeks started to return.

When she lifted her chin, her eyes were filled with tears. 'Don't do this. Don't be like this.' Her head went from one brother to the other. 'I hate this too. But Mamma and Papà want us to work together. They want us to be a family.' She turned to face Giovanni. 'You've read the will, but I think we should have a little time to consider what it all means.' She let go of Leo's hand and reached for his shoulders, turning him to face her. 'Leo, I want to know you. I want to know my brother. I've already missed out on so much of your life, I don't want to miss out on any more. I'm not asking you to be my best friend. But family is important to me—now, more than ever.' She squeezed his shoulders. 'Why don't you both take a bit of time? This is a lot, I know that—for all of us. We all need to think—to process—and…' she glanced at Sebastian again '…probably to cool off. How about we agree to meet again later?'

Her eyes were pleading as she looked between the two men. Giovanni nodded. 'Sounds reasonable. Nothing will happen quickly in terms of the will. It will take around six to eight weeks for things to be legally tied up back in Italy, and I can string things out as long as you all need.'

'Fine.' Sebastian's answer was short.

'We can meet again around Christmastime?' Noemi said, her voice breaking with distress. 'Back here?' She pressed her lips together. 'It's what Mamma and Papà always wanted.'

There was an edge to her words. A hint of desperation. It brought it home to him again. She'd just lost her parents. They all had.

He moved from her grasp and collected his coat. The swell of emotion in the room too much for him. He gave the briefest of nods. 'I'll get back to you both,' he said as he walked swiftly towards the glass doors and out into the dark night.

He hadn't even bothered to fasten his coat again and the Swiss Alpine air bit around him. He could barely register the cold, his body was so flushed with heat.

New York. That's where Leo wanted to be right now. That was where he called home. He'd left Indiana and his adoptive parents behind a long time ago.

As he tramped along the snow-covered path he quickly realised he had no idea where he was going. The car from the airport had dropped his luggage at the luxury chalet booked by his PA. Trouble was, he didn't know where that was. He pulled out his phone to search on a map. Around him people were crowding out of bars and hotels. It only took a few glances to realise that the Mont Coeur ski resort was filled with the rich, the very rich and the very, very rich.

He knew how ironic that thought was. He was in that category—as was his newfound family. But Leo didn't usually willingly mix in these circles. He'd always been picky about who he surrounded himself with, preferring people with their feet firmly on the ground to those who worried about climbing the social ladder.

He could go into a bar—find somewhere to have a drink. But he wasn't really in the mood for a drink. Distraction maybe—but not a drink.

He checked out the map on his phone and headed down another street, this one a little quieter and leading away from the main thoroughfare.

He probably should have hired a car or tried to find a taxi, as he realised the road towards his luxury chalet was mainly uphill. But the truth was he didn't really mind. It gave him a little time to think about what had just happened.

Several things burned in his mind. Giovanni had said the will had always included him. That made him feel…odd. His adoptive parents had always maintained that his real parents couldn't wait to be rid of him. The harsh words had felt as if they'd burned their way into his soul, wounding him in a way he'd never spoken about. He'd spent years resenting both his real and his adoptive parents, feeling as if he wasn't really wanted anywhere. Finding out now that was all untrue was more unsettling than he could have ever imagined.

He let out a long, slow breath, sending warm air out into the icy night, clouding around him.

Leo reached the end of the street and looked up from the map on his phone. His chalet should be off to the right, but to his left he saw Mont Coeur's practice slopes. Even though it was nine o'clock at night, there were still a few people getting in that last run.

They were illuminated with bright white lights, reflecting off the glossy snow, smoothed down hard by the constant traffic on the slopes. In most other ski resorts, the slopes were high above the actual towns. Mont Coeur was different. It was built halfway up the mountain, almost right in the middle of the slopes, which made them much more accessible.

He stopped for a minute, leaning on a fence

as he watched a single figure head down towards him. Dressed completely in black, the figure zig-zagged down the practically empty slope at an alarming rate of speed. Skiing was something he'd loved to do over the years and he could appreciate the skill and expertise. He frowned. Wasn't the figure coming down just a little too fast?

There was a loud bang to his right. His head flicked to the side, just in time to see a car with a black cloud of smoke coming from under its bonnet.

He flicked back to the skier. *Oh, no.*

They'd turned to check out the noise too, and now it was too late. In the blink of an eye he realised they hadn't slowed their descent enough. That split-second distraction had been too much.

They desperately tried to slow, but it was too little, too late and they hurtled into the tyres at the bottom of the practice slope with a sickening crash.

Leo didn't think twice. He leapt over the fence and scrambled over the thick tyres. There was hardly anyone around, and it was clear he was the closest.

The figure was lying crumpled on the ground, skis askew and one of their legs in an awkward position. Leo slipped and slid on the snow. 'Are you okay? Can I do something to help you?'

He knelt down next to the figure in black. Now he was closer he could see it was a woman. The black salopettes and padded ski jacket couldn't hide the slim curves underneath. She still hadn't responded. He touched her arm, 'Hi, I'm Leo. Can I help you?'

There was a groan underneath him. The twisted leg moved and she gave a yelp. *'Foitrottl!'*

He smiled. He may not have understood the language—was it Swiss? German?—but he understood the sentiment. Not quite as ladylike as he might have imagined. 'Well, at least I know you're conscious,' he said.

Her arms shot upwards and she snapped the fastener on her ski helmet and pushed her ski goggles upwards, revealing a mass of ice blonde hair.

'What on earth was that noise?' she said, switching to English. She was mad. She was more than mad.

Leo couldn't help but smile again. As well as the avalanche of blonde hair, this lady had the clearest blue eyes he'd ever seen. She pretty much looked like some kind of ice princess but he could already guess how she would take that kind of comparison.

'It sounded like a combination of a car back-firing and an engine blowing up. Either way, it was loud.'

She was digging her elbows into the snow and struggling to push herself up.

'Can I give you hand?' He stood up and reached out towards her.

For a second he thought she might refuse, but after the briefest pause she pulled one hand from her glove and grasped his fingers tightly.

He tugged—maybe a little more firmly than he needed to—and pulled her straight up into him. His other arm caught around her waist just as her weight hit her feet and she yelped again as her leg buckled beneath her.

He tightened his grip and pulled her against his hip. 'Do you think something's broken? Do you want me to call an ambulance for you?'

She was breathing hard and fast but her skin was pale. 'Just give me a second,' she gasped.

So he did. And even though it was freezing after a few seconds he was struck by the heat emanating from her slight frame. She was taller than most women he met, but still at least six inches shorter than him. He stood silently, watching a little colour appear in her pale cheeks and her breathing eventually starting to slow. She was holding her left foot off the ground and tentatively put it back down, wincing almost immediately.

'Want me to carry you?'

Her frown was fierce but she didn't bite his head off. Instead she leaned a little into him. 'Nope, definitely not. Sorry to be a pest, but I've got a bit of an old injury. Would you mind just helping me limp back to the ski hut? There's a buggy I can use there to get back to my chalet.'

'Can you stand for a second?' She nodded and he bent to retrieve her skis and poles before sliding his arm back around her waist and taking some of her weight. 'Okay, then. What were you doing, practising so late? Most people are in the town by now.'

She gripped onto his arm with her other hand as she limped alongside him, being careful not to put too much weight on her foot.

Leo couldn't help but ask again. 'You're sure that's not broken?'

She shook her head. 'I'm sure. Believe me. I've broken a few bones in my time.'

It was just the way she said it. He couldn't help himself. 'What—yours or other people's?'

She threw back her head and laughed, then obviously put too much weight on her bad foot. 'Ouch.'

Leo actions were instinctual. He dropped the skis, bent down and swept her up into his arms.

'What are you doing?' Her eyes were wide. She glanced around but it was late, the slopes were quiet, and there wasn't really anyone else watching.

'I'm carrying you,' he said simply. He strode towards the large ski hut. 'No point hurting yourself when you don't need to. I'll come back for those in a second,' he said, noticing as she craned over his shoulder to look for her abandoned equipment. He looked down at her curiously. He could tell she was just about to object again. 'So, have you broken a lot of bones? What are you—a ski instructor?'

There was a flash of something on her face as they approached the ski hut. She sighed. 'Yes, I guess I am.'

He moved around the side of the building. Just like she'd said, there was a large SUV with snow tyres. 'Want me to drive?' he asked as he set her gently down next to the passenger door.

'Will you carry me round to the other side if I say no?' she quipped.

Leo smiled. Whatever else had happened today, things were definitely looking up. He winked at her. 'Your wish is my command, Ice Princess.'

\* \* \*

Ice Princess? Had he actually just called her Ice Princess?

If she had been feeling herself she'd toss her head and stomp off. Trouble was, she wasn't feeling herself. She actually felt as if she might be sick all over her ski boots.

As her rescuer disappeared to retrieve her skis and poles, she wondered if maybe it was the shock of the noise of the backfiring car. Maybe it was her current feeling of stupidity for allowing herself to be distracted when she really should know better. Or maybe it was that whole host of memories that had come flooding back as she'd tumbled down the slope, too quickly and completely out of control.

She dug into her ski jacket and pulled out her key. As he returned, leaning her equipment against the SUV, she steeled herself to say words she'd never thought she would. 'Actually, would you mind? I promise I only live a five-minute drive from here.'

The guy—Leo he'd said he was called—gave a quick nod as she pressed the button to open the doors. 'Not at all,' he said graciously.

He was being a gentleman. There was obviously a cheeky demeanour hiding under there, but for now she'd take the gentleman. Anything to get home as soon as possible.

She slid into her seat, suddenly aware she'd been a little rude. 'And it's Anissa—not Ice Princess.'

He smiled as he slid into the driver's seat and pressed the button to start the engine. 'Anissa.' He gave a nod of approval. 'Sounds like a kind of ice princess name to me.'

'Do you know *many* ice princesses, Leo?'

He laughed and held out his hand. 'Leo Baxter. From New York. Just here for a few days on...' his face gave a little twist '...family business.'

She shook his hand. 'Anissa Lang. And this Ice Princess has the illustrious other titles of part-time ski instructor, part-time chalet maid.' He smiled. He had a nice smile, dark, curly hair a little longer than average and bright blue eyes that could stop a girl in her tracks. Just as well she was sitting down. She held his gaze just a few seconds longer than she meant to.

He didn't look away. His grin just got wider and she felt colour rush into her cheeks. What on earth was she doing? She took a deep breath and focused on the view through the windscreen instead. It was safer.

He pulled the car out of the parking lot and stopped at the road junction.

'Right.' She pointed.

'Were you doing a lesson?' he queried. 'I didn't notice any students on the slopes with you.'

She shook her head. 'Too late for lessons. And students wouldn't be allowed on that slope. Too dangerous.'

He gave a nod of his head as he continued down the dark road. 'You don't say.'

A wave of nausea rushed over her and she put a hand to her mouth. 'You okay?' he asked quickly, his cheeky quips instantly replaced by concern.

She swallowed and pointed a little further down the road. 'Take the next left, please. I'm just at the end of that road.'

She leaned back against the seat and gave a sigh. 'Maybe I hit my head. I'm feeling a bit queasy.'

His eyes were laced with concern, but he didn't say anything else until he pulled up outside her staff chalet. A few seconds later he'd stopped the car, jumped out, rounded the car and opened her door. 'Let's get you inside. Maybe if you sit down for a few minutes and get some water, you'll feel a little better. If you don't, I'm sure I can find a doctor in the resort to check you over.'

She really wanted to argue with him, but getting inside her chalet seemed like the priority right now, so she let him help her out and up the steps to the chalet, not even objecting when he took the key from her slightly shaking hand and opened the door for her. He flicked on her lights and slid his arm around her waist, helping her inside.

She sagged down onto her sofa in relief, unzipping her ski jacket and taking a few deep breaths. When she opened her eyes a few seconds later, Leo had already started the fire.

'Well, if I'm Ice Princess, you must be Prince Charming.' She smiled.

It was odd. She didn't feel threatened by the complete stranger who was currently inside her temporary home and finding his way around. She was actually feeling relieved there was someone else with her right now.

'Oh,' she said in surprise as he sat down on the coffee table opposite her and lifted up her ski boot.

Those blue eyes twinkled. 'Prince Charming? Isn't that the guy obsessed with shoes? Let's get these ski boots off and you can see if you've done any damage.' He really was too handsome for his own good.

He undid the clips, loosened the boot then gave it a gentle tug, pulling it off. She clenched her jaw, waiting for wave of pain she'd normally feel if she'd done some damage. There were a few twinges but nothing severe.

He pulled off the other boot, holding her foot for a little longer than necessary. 'Okay?' His question seemed sincere, so she nodded as he moved so her feet could rest on the table in front of her. 'You still look really pale.' He glanced around the room. 'How about something medicinal? I think you're in a bit of shock. Do you have any brandy?'

Her brain really couldn't think straight. Brandy. Yes. She had some of that. She waved her hand. 'Cabinet behind you.'

Two minutes later she heard the clink of glasses. She leaned forward and peeled down her socks. No obvious swelling. Thank goodness. She gave both of her feet a cautious circle. Whilst one was definitely sore, it wasn't as bad as she'd initially feared.

A glass was pressed into her hand and Leo lowered himself into the seat next to her.

She took a sip of the brandy and pulled a face. 'I'm not sure if giving someone alcohol for shock is really the official treatment.' She gave her head a shake. 'You know, St Bernards don't really have brandy around their necks.'

He smiled and raised his glass. 'What can I say? I've always been one for old wives' tales.'

She looked at him curiously. His face was a tiny bit flushed in her rapidly warming chalet, but there was no question that this was one of the most handsome guys she'd seen in a while. Mont Coeur was no stranger to numerous jet-set playboy millionaires, but he didn't seem quite the type. She took another sip of her brandy, which warmed on the way down.

'I'm not sure I believe you—you don't look like an old-wives'-tales kind of guy.' She sighed. 'But then again, I'm not the type of girl to let a stranger drive her car—or come into her chalet—so I guess it's just a night of firsts.'

There was a definite twinkle in his eye. She nudged him.

At any other time alarm bells would be going off in her head. But the one thing she instantly felt around this guy was safe. That was it. He had a safe kind of smile. She liked that—that and those bright blue eyes. 'Want to take that wool coat off before you die from heat exhaustion?'

Her heart skipped a few beats. Had she really just said that? More or less invited him to stay a bit longer?

Deep down something was flickering inside her—and it was nothing to do with the fire. Everything about this was so out of character for her. Under normal circumstances she would probably have tried to hound her rescuer back outside the door. But Leo just seemed… different.

There was something in his eyes that she couldn't quite figure. He had the tiniest air of mystery around him—that and a whole load of sex appeal. A lethal combination.

He laughed, unfastened the coat and shrugged it off. 'A night of firsts,' he repeated. There was a strange kind of look on his face. 'I guess it's certainly been one of those.'

There it was—the air of mystery that just seemed to reel her in. She turned a little towards him. 'What do you mean?'

He shook his head. 'Let's just say I'm glad of the distraction.'

Now she was definitely curious. 'Well, from my experience, most people come to Mont Coeur to either ski or...' she raised her eyebrows '...to show off how rich they are. Which category are you in?'

For a second he was silent, then he took a long, slow swig from the brandy glass. 'I can just about hold my own on a ski slope. But I've never skied at Mont Coeur before. I came here at kind of short notice. I didn't bring any equipment with me.'

'So you didn't come here for the skiing?'

He shook his head. He really wasn't giving much away. But the way that he looked at her through those heavy-lidded eyes, it was making her stomach do a whole lot of flip-flops. Never mind skiing. Right now her stomach thought she was a gymnast.

'But you were watching tonight?'

He nodded. 'I've only been here a few hours. I haven't even reached my...' he put his fingers in the air '..."luxury cabin" yet.'

Anissa's stomach gave a little twist. *Please don't let him be staying in one of the cabins I'm cleaning.*

'So, is it business or pleasure?' She licked her lips, a little nervous at asking the question. For all she knew, he could actually be here with a wife or fiancée, and really only was being gentlemanly by helping her home. She unintentionally held her breath as she waited for the answer.

'I imagine some people would expect me to say a bit of both.' He gave another sigh. 'But the honest answer is neither. In a lot of ways, I wish I'd never come. There's nothing I'd like more than to jump back on the soonest flight to New York.'

Her stomach gave a little pang. The first interesting guy she'd met in a long time couldn't wait to get out of Dodge. Typical.

But it was the way he'd said the words that mattered. As if they made him sad. 'Then why don't you?' she asked quietly.

He met her gaze with his blue eyes. 'Because

I'm a bit in limbo. What I do next could affect other people—whether I like it or not.'

Empathy swelled within her. Connection. Because those words were so familiar to her. What she did wouldn't affect anyone other than herself. But being in limbo? She raised her glass to him. 'Limbo. I see your few days' worth of limbo and raise you a whole year's worth.'

He turned closer towards her, leaning in and letting her see the shadow on his jawline and the tiny lines around his eyes. That tiny movement made her catch her breath at what might lie ahead. The woody scent of his aftershave filled her senses. She liked it. It had a hint of spice mixed with earthy tones.

He leaned his head on one hand and gave her a sexy kind of smile. 'How did a gorgeous girl like you end up in limbo in Mont Coeur? Have you always lived here?'

Gorgeous. He'd just called her gorgeous. She could almost hear the echoing voices of approval of her fellow chalet maids at her rapidly rising heart rate. For months they'd been telling her to pay more attention to the guys around her. For months she'd told them she had other priorities and that no one had captured her attention. And they hadn't. Until now.

She shook her head and tried her best to play it cool. 'I'm Austrian. But I've spent most of my life on skis, no matter where I've lived.' She lifted one hand. 'This last year? Let's just say it hasn't been my best—hasn't been my favourite. Limbo is exactly the right word to describe the last twelve months of my life.'

It hurt. Every memory about it still hurt. From the physical pain of crashing down a mountainside. To the psychological pain of realising her hopes of winning an international skiing championship gold medal had just been ripped from her grasp. Then there was the emotional trauma of her fiancé *and* coach, Alain, dumping her.

Leo reached out and grabbed her hand, the touch of his warm skin shooting an instant tingle up her arm. His voice was deep. His other hand reached over and tucked a wayward strand of hair behind her ear. It was a personal touch, an intimate touch, and the skin on her face was on fire with it. 'How about, for one night only, we try and forget about the stuff that's dragging us down?'

She blinked. Had he actually just said that?

The fire was flickering behind him, sending a warm glow around the room. Her heart missed a few beats.

No way. She wouldn't. Not ever. She wasn't that kind of girl.

But…

Somehow, tonight, she wanted to be.

She really, really wanted to be.

She prayed her voice wouldn't shake as she uttered the words. 'I could live with forgetting about everything dragging me down.'

He moved closer, his mouth only a few inches from hers, and she licked her lips in anticipation.

She paused for the briefest second. 'Promise me you have no wife, no fiancée, no girlfriend.'

He gave a flicker of smile. 'Promise. What about you?'

She smiled too as she leaned in. 'Oh, I don't have a wife, a fiancée or a girlfriend.' This was reaching the teasing stage. Her favourite part.

He smiled back as he reached up and slid his fingers through her hair, anchoring his hand at the back of her head. 'No significant other?'

She shook her head. 'No significant other.'

His lips brushed against her ear. 'Then how about we get ourselves distracted?'

She must be crazy. She must be losing her mind. But for the first time in a year all she could think about was how good it felt to be in the arms of this man she found wildly attractive and how in control she felt. She was making this decision. No one was doing it for her. Leo Baxter was hot.

And he was all hers.

This was one night. Everything else she could worry about tomorrow.

She smiled as she brushed her lips against his. 'So…distract me.'

# CHAPTER TWO

LEO BLINKED AS he heard the faint noise of someone shuffling around. There was only a tiny glimmer of light outside. The bed was uncomfortable and his mind took a few seconds to orientate itself.

Mont Coeur. The will. Sebastian. Noemi.

And then there was last night. Anissa.

He rolled over and leaned on one arm. Sure enough, Anissa was padding around the room, pulling on some kind of uniform.

She looked up. 'Sorry, didn't mean to wake you. I have an early shift.'

He wasn't one for overnight stays and awkward next mornings. Seemed like he'd had more firsts than he'd expected to. The jet lag and emotional trauma of last night had obviously just wiped him out.

He watched as she pulled her hair up into a ponytail. He'd thought she'd looked good last night, but even early in the morning she looked good. Something twinged inside him and his gaze connected with hers.

This was where things got uncomfortable. This was where he had to make a hasty exit and try and find the luxury chalet he'd never made it to last night.

He glanced around the room, trying to find his clothes. Anissa pulled on her jacket and Leo instantly swung his legs from the bed. She had to leave. And she wouldn't want to leave a stranger in her house.

'Give me a second to grab my things and I'll get out of your hair.'

Images of last night flashed through his brain as he pulled on his shirt and trousers. Good images. Great images. And a connection he'd never thought he'd feel.

Anissa was standing at the bedroom door, watching him a little awkwardly. She sucked in a breath. 'Thanks for helping me last night.'

He pushed his feet into his shoes and moved closer. 'You're welcome. How's your foot this morning?'

She gave it a little stamp. 'A bit sore, but that's it.'

Maybe she hadn't realised it but she was blocking his exit to the door. He stopped in front of her. 'Last night was…' He let his voice tail off, unsure how exactly to end the sentence.

'The best sex I've had in years.'

He blinked, then laughed. It seemed that Anissa had no problem finishing the sentence for him. 'Okay, then…' he gave his head a shake at her quick words '… I guess I'd have to agree with that.'

Her blue eyes were fixed on his. His stomach gave a twist. Please don't let this be something it isn't.

His brain was all over the place right now, as were his emotions. In the space of a few months he'd found his parents, lost his parents, met a brother and sister he'd never known and been blackmailed into taking an interest in the family business. He didn't have room for anything else right now.

'I'm not looking for romance.' Anissa spoke quickly.

'Neither am I.' The answer came out automatically, with a sense of relief.

'And I never usually do anything like this,' she added. 'So please don't think this is normal for me. Last night was just…' This time it was her that couldn't find the words to complete the sentence.

'A one-off,' he finished for her.

She nodded in agreement. 'A one-off.'

They were still close. Close enough that he could smell the fruity shampoo from her hair that she'd pulled into a ponytail high on her head.

It would be so easy to lean forward and kiss her. To capture those lips in his again and pull her back down onto the unmade bed.

The truth was Anissa hadn't been wrong. Last night had unexpectedly been the best night of his life. But in reality he hardly knew her. And his timing was terrible.

She stood back against the door to let him pass. The early morning light was filtering through the windows of the small staff chalet. It was small, neat and functional, with only a few hints of the woman who actually stayed here. A framed photo of her standing in her skis, the two brandy glasses from last night, the ski boots still lying on the living-room floor. He was struck with how much it didn't really look like a home. The similarities between this place and his own penthouse apartment in New York sent a wash of recognition over him. How long had she said she'd been here? A year?

He picked up his coat and fastened it. Anissa moved in front of him and held out her hand towards him. 'It was nice to meet you, Leo Baxter.'

Her body was rigid, and she was being formal, but he could still sense the hint of humour in her eyes.

He slipped his warm hand into hers. 'It was nice to meet you too, Anissa Lang.' Her handshake was firm and he found himself in no hurry to let go. Her pale blue eyes were fixed on his.

His heart twisted at the first flicker of a connection he'd felt in, oh, so long. He tilted his head a little to the side. He wasn't sentimental. Never had been. Never would be—especially after recent events. But there was something about this girl beyond the obvious beauty and the passion she'd sparked in him last night. He gave a wry smile. 'Bad timing, but in another world, another place I would have very much liked to know you better.' He pulled her towards him and dropped a kiss on her cheek.

And before she had a chance to reply he turned on his heel and left quickly, walking out into the fresh snow and the rapidly wakening resort.

He had so much to think about. So much to consider.

And he didn't have a single clue what he really wanted to do.

Anissa held up the rota again. 'Oh, come on, someone swap with me. *Please.*'

Lucy leaned over Anissa's shoulder and looked at the list of occupiers in the most luxurious chalets in the whole resort. 'What's wrong with Leo Baxter, then? Bad breath? Wandering hands? Suggestive comments?'

Heat rushed into Anissa's cheeks.

Chloe laughed as she straightened her uniform next to them. 'Oh, no, none of that.' Then she glanced sideways at Anissa and shrugged. 'Or maybe two out of the three.' She laughed. 'But, hey, who doesn't want to go to the chalet of the gorgeous billionaire Anissa snagged a few nights ago?'

Lucy's eyes widened. '*That* was the guy?' She laughed too and shook her head. 'Oh, no way. I'm not swapping.' She pointed at Anissa. 'You've gotta go clean the hottie's chalet.' She swept up her equipment. 'And who knows what might happen—again!' she added with a wicked wink.

Anissa's stomach turned over as her colleagues left. Darn it. She'd managed to get out of cleaning Leo's chalet the last few days as she'd been working with other girls. But she'd made the mistake of telling Chloe all about her mystery encounter and great night before she'd realised Leo was actually staying in one of the chalets she was supposed to service.

She checked her watch. She had another chalet to clean too. Maybe she could time things just right and manage to avoid Leo. He was here for…business, wasn't he? Chances were he would be out at some point during the day.

She gathered her equipment and headed out towards the chalets. There was a large red SUV outside the one that a family was staying in, and nothing outside Leo's.

She licked her dry lips and headed towards his, turning the key carefully in the lock as her stomach did somersaults. 'Housekeeping,' she called. 'Anyone home?'

Her voice echoed around her. She stayed frozen for a few seconds, wondering if there'd be any delayed response, but after a minute she breathed a sigh of relief and closed the door behind her, looking around carefully.

Chalet was a bit of a misnomer. It might suit the place in which she lived, but it didn't suit these massive luxury houses halfway up the slopes. She grabbed some of her cleaning equipment. The people who stayed here were millionaires at a minimum. They expected impeccable service. And as the chalet had seventeen rooms, this wasn't somewhere you could whip round with a brush and duster in half an hour.

Her heart started to race in her chest. She really needed to use this window of opportunity wisely. She had to get in, and out, as soon as possible. Her brain tried to think logically. There was no way Leo was using all these rooms. Chances were she would have the main room, a bedroom, bathroom and kitchen to clean. She could do that before he got back. At least she hoped she could.

She automatically plugged in a fresh scented atomiser. It was changed every day—probably just to let the guests know that the chalet had been serviced. She grabbed her mop and bucket and dashed up the stairs to do a quick check around. None of the rooms on the top floor looked as if they'd been touched—everything was still pristine.

She ran down to the next floor. Leo was using the master suite. No surprise there. But it felt a little strange, walking into a room and seeing his belongings scattered around. The white bed was rumpled and unmade. She walked over and touched it, then pulled her hand back. It was weird. She was used to making strangers' beds, picking up their clothes and folding them, restocking their bathrooms and kitchens. But this wasn't a stranger. This was Leo. The guy who'd made her forget a year of feeling unloved and unwanted. A guy who'd actually made her feel attractive and sexy again.

She could smell him in this room. That woody aftershave he'd been wearing when he'd been with her, the way his stubble had scraped along her jaw...

She took a breath and sat down for a second on the bed. She'd been here a year and she'd never behaved like this. What on earth was wrong with her? What had changed the other night?

Even this, sitting on one of guest's beds, was something she would never do. She glanced around, almost expecting there to be hidden cameras taping this terrible misdemeanour. She ran her hand over the bed sheet. Leo had slept here last night. Had he thought about her? Had she even crossed his mind?

What if someone else had shared the bed with him? She jumped back up, annoyed that her thoughts had even gone there. It was enough to bring her back to her senses.

She started stripping off the sheets, remaking the bed with clean sheets in record time. She wiped around the room with a damp duster, picking up a discarded shirt and pair of trousers and hanging them up. The bathroom was messier. He'd managed to get toothpaste and shaving foam all over the sink. And all four towels were lying on the bathroom floor, indicating they should be replaced.

What was it with guys and towels?

Anissa worked as quickly as she could. Normally she would take longer, ensuring the glass shower door was smear free and the mirror completely spotless. But that would all take time she wasn't sure she had. A quick wipe would have to do.

She hurried down to the kitchen and started to clean there, scrubbing a little harder than necessary in some places. Her eyes kept glancing at the door. She really wasn't doing the job she normally did but she was willing to risk a complaint if it meant she could avoid coming face to face with Leo again.

Darn it. She picked up the discarded coffee pods. She'd forgotten the hamper to restock the kitchen.

There was noise outside and she turned in time to see a large black SUV pull up directly outside. *Oh, no.*

She gathered the towels and bed sheets in her arms, looking first one way then the other. Normally she would just put these in a black laundry bag and phone for them to be collected. But all of a sudden she thought about darting out the back door and taking them back to the service office herself. She looked at the back door again.

But it was too late. Her jumbled brain had waited too long.

Leo was at the door.

* * *

He'd met with Giovanni again. He'd called his own lawyers in New York, desperately trying to find any possible way to get out of looking after the family business for the next six months. But things were not looking good—and unless he wanted to ruin the Cattaneo family business, staying was beginning to look like a distinct possibility.

As Leo opened the door of the chalet he was struck by the fresh scent of pines and cinnamon. A hint of Christmas. A clear sign that the chalet service had visited.

Then he stopped. And blinked.

'Anissa?'

She was standing near the kitchen, a white pile of something in her arms. Her cheeks flushed pink instantly. Something she'd said the night they'd met pricked in his brain.

'You work here?'

'I… I… I…'

She was clearly flustered.

'I know you said you were a chalet maid, but I didn't realise you worked in these chalets.' He was surprised to see her. And even more surprised by the fact his heart was missing a few rapid beats.

He saw her swallow nervously. 'You didn't say where you were staying—'

'I didn't know,' he cut in. He gave a laugh. 'I hadn't made it to my chalet before we met.'

A frown creased her brow and she stared at him for a few seconds with her pale blue eyes. 'Of course,' she said softly.

He moved towards her. 'Hey, why don't you dump that stuff and have a coffee with me?'

Something flitted across her eyes. 'I can't. I have another chalet to clean. And I haven't really finished in here.' She pulled a face as she glanced back at the kitchen. 'You might not even have coffee. I haven't replenished your supplies in the kitchen.'

He stepped even closer. As he breathed he felt a wave of familiarity. A scent. Her scent. The fruity one he'd smelt a few days ago. Orange blossom. The sensations from the other night flooded back. Her warmth. Her passion. The spark in her eye.

For the past few days he'd been buried beneath a mountain of legal stuff. Now, seeing Anissa again, it just made him regret the choice he'd made. He'd liked the way she'd distracted him. He'd more than liked it. And he kind of wished he could capture it all again.

He gave a smile. 'Hey, what happened to my brilliant chalet maid, then? The one who stocks up the coffee varieties every day, along with all the fresh bread and chocolate-chip cookies.'

Anissa let out a little laugh. She shook her head. 'Yeah. You've had Rena the last few days, but she's off now.' She shrugged. 'And you got me. The poor excuse of chalet maid. Sorry.'

She moved to the side. 'Give me a sec.' She walked over and dumped the laundry in a black fabric sack and sat it outside the front door. She dialled a number on the phone and spoke for a few seconds before replacing the handset and turning back around to face him.

'Okay, the restock hamper will be here in a few minutes. Don't worry, you'll have coffee.'

He gave a nod as his heart gave a little trip. 'And will you join me?'

She glanced at her watch then gave a small smile. 'Okay, a quick one. I do have a day job— no matter how much I don't want one.'

He raised his eyebrows in interest. Perfect. Anissa Lang was going to distract him. Again.

Her stomach was in knots. For the first few seconds she'd just wanted to run. Talk about embarrassing. The guy she'd spent a red-hot night with had just found her changing his towels. Hardly a great moment.

But it was odd. Leo had made her feel instantly at ease. And there was definitely still… something. It didn't matter that it had been a few days and she'd been deliberately avoiding him. It only took being in his presence again for a few seconds to feel that buzz, feel that attraction. And she wasn't imagining the sparkle in his eyes. For some crazy reason she liked being around this guy. And—no matter what some people might think—it was nothing to do with his billionaire status.

A few minutes later the supplies arrived in a wicker hamper. She unpacked the coffee, the bread, the milk and the cookies. Leo was at her elbow the whole time, starting the coffee machine, putting in the pods and lifting out the cookies.

The clients who stayed in these chalets were well taken care of. They could pre-order fresh deliveries for every day. Anissa was kind of surprised at Leo's response to everything in the hamper. 'Didn't you order all this stuff?'

He shook his head. 'No. Why? Can you do that?'

Anissa shook her head. 'Sure you can. Didn't you book this place?'

Leo pulled a face. 'Ah…maybe not.'

'So, who booked it for you? Your family?'

He shook his head. 'No. My PA.'

'Oh, of course.' Anissa smiled and rolled her eyes. 'The PA. Well, here's hoping she ordered what you like, and not what she likes.'

'I'm easy to please,' he said quickly.

'That's what they all say,' she joked.

Something flickered across his eyes and her heart sank. She touched his arm. 'No.' She shook her head and pulled a face. 'Absolutely, no. That's not what I meant.' Her heart was beating wildly in her chest. She breathed slowly and met his gaze. 'I told you. I never did that before.'

His bright blue eyes were fixed on hers. This guy could complain about her. This guy could cost her the job that she didn't even really love.

He blinked. 'I believe you. Now, what do you take in your coffee?'

A wave of relief swept over her. Thank goodness. She'd hate it if he thought she just jumped into bed with every guy she met. Some chalet maids had that kind of reputation and Anissa didn't want him to think of her like that.

She picked up the milk from the counter. 'Just this.' His fingers brushed against hers as he took the carton from her hand and splashed the milk into the cups. 'Want a cookie too?' He lifted the pack as he headed towards the table.

She shook her head. 'You missed out. The oatmeal and raisin are the superior cookie here, but everyone seems to order the chocolate chip.'

He raised his eyebrows as he sat down. 'Ah… insider secrets. Thanks. I'll order oatmeal and raisin tomorrow.'

She pulled out the chair opposite and sat down. This was a little weird. A little formal. Last time they'd been in each other's company he'd been pulling off her boots and sitting next to her on the sofa.

'How's your leg?'

She shrugged. 'Okay. I strapped it up the last few days when I was doing lessons.'

He leaned his head on one hand, his fingers threading through his dark tousled hair as he sipped his coffee. 'How long have you skied for?'

'Practically since I could breathe. I'm Austrian. It's in my genes. The other day on the slopes? That was stupid of me. I lost my concentration. I never do that. Never.'

The last time she'd lost her concentration it had cost her a chance at the gold medal. She'd been stupid. The effects had meant her whole world had come crashing down around her. And she'd spent the last year trying desperately to reach the same level she'd been at before. But it didn't seem to matter how hard she practised, it was still out of her reach. The accident the other night had shaken her more than she could admit. If Leo hadn't been there to help her, then distract her...

He gave a slow, thoughtful nod. 'Maybe you had other things on your mind?'

'Like you have?'

She couldn't pretend not to notice that far-off look he got in his eyes.

He met her gaze and smiled. 'Am I that obvious?'

She sipped her coffee. 'Just a little.'

He nodded again. 'I thought I would have been back in New York by now.'

Her stomach gave a little flip. If Leo had gone back to New York she wouldn't have seen him again. It surprised her how much she didn't like that idea.

'Why aren't you?'

He bit his bottom lip. It was clear he was trying to find the right words. 'Family...issues. The matter I came to deal with should only have taken a day. But there's been...complications. And it seems I can't get away when I thought I could.'

He ran his fingers through his rumpled hair. She could tell just by looking how tense he was. The muscles around his neck and shoulders looked tight. His forehead marred by a deep furrow. And he looked tired. Like he hadn't really slept properly.

She could tell something was wrong. For the first time he seemed a little awkward. It was obvious the family stuff was getting to him.

Her heart gave a little tug. She remembered

feeling as if things were pressing down around about her—in fact, it sort of resembled the whole last year for her. But a few days ago she'd met a gorgeous mystery man who'd pulled her out of her slump. Leo.

'It's a good time of year to be in Mont Coeur,' she said.

He looked up and gave an amused smile. 'It seems like it's Christmas already here.'

She shrugged. 'From what I hear, New York is pretty much the same.'

'Okay, I'll give you that.'

She waved her hand. 'Anyway, I was talking about the slopes, not the Christmas decorations.' She put her hands around her coffee cup and looked up at him. 'You should try them. Skiing at night—it's peaceful. It's calming.' She gave a smile, 'And the slopes are much quieter. Maybe it will help clear your head a little?'

He was watching her with those bright blue eyes. 'Are you asking me on a date?'

She laughed out loud as she felt heat rush into her cheeks. 'Nope. I was making a suggestion. You said you didn't have equipment, but I can tell you where to hire some. And it's good stuff.'

'Could be dangerous up on the slopes alone at night.' His eyes were twinkling.

'What are you suggesting?'

He gave a careless shrug. 'Well, you know. I was thinking that someone could come with me. It would be much safer. After all, I've seen you on the slopes. You might need rescuing again.'

'Ha!' She sucked in a breath in mock horror. 'Mr Baxter, that almost seems like an insult.'

He raised his eyebrows. 'How about, Ms Lang, you take it as a challenge?'

He let the words hang in the air between them. She liked this. She liked his humour. She pushed herself up from the chair. If she didn't get to the next chalet soon she would end up in trouble.

'Okay then. As a resident here, why don't I show you why the world loves Mont Coeur so much? Do you have any other plans for tonight?'

He shook his head. 'None. I'm all yours.'

'Then how about we meet later—around nine o'clock?' She grabbed a notepad sitting next to the phone. 'Here's the name and number of the place to hire gear. Okay?'

His hand touched hers as she slid the piece of paper across the table towards him. He smiled again. 'This sounds like a date,' he said, his tone teasing.

She shook her head. 'It's no date.' She wagged her finger at him as she headed to the door.

'Don't you be getting any ideas, Leo Baxter.' She gave him a cheeky wink and then hurried out the door before her rapidly beating heart exploded in her chest.

The hand he'd just touched was pressed up against her chest wall, still tingling. She looked down and smiled.

What on earth had she just done?

# CHAPTER THREE

Leo Baxter was used to being in control. Anything else was alien to him. Which meant the last few months had thrown him off his game.

The letter he'd received from his birth parents was still in his briefcase. It had been there since it had landed in his penthouse mailbox in August. It had taken him weeks to reply, and then, when he had, his mother and father had sounded overjoyed and couldn't wait to come to New York to meet him.

He'd been struggling with the realisation that what he'd believed for most of his life had been wrong when they'd died in a helicopter crash on way to New York. He'd never even got to see them in the flesh. He'd never got to hug them. He'd never got a kiss from them. It was almost as if, since he'd received that letter, all elements of his normally micromanaged existence had spiralled out of his control.

The will was just another element. He hated

being manipulated. He hated the thought that someone might be trying to take charge of his life.

His parents had had no idea where he was, or how life had turned out for him, when they'd included him in the will. Maybe they'd hoped it would give him the financial security that most people craved. But Leo had no need of financial security from his parents. He'd carved out his own successful business through dedication, hard work and a tiny edge of ruthlessness.

If they'd had a chance to meet they would have realised that Leo didn't need money. He had no need to be part of the family business—or any interest in it. But that chance had been stolen from them all, and right now the will was creating havoc with his own business interests.

He needed to be in New York. He had several large deals coming off and for Leo the devil was in the detail. The thing he prided himself on. Being in Mont Coeur, surrounded by family pressure, was messing with his head.

Anissa's idea to come up the mountain to clear his head had come at the perfect time.

There was a nudge at his back. 'Come on, then, Leo. Show me your moves.'

She'd arrived behind him right on time at the ski lift. Her eyes swept up and down his body. 'Did you get that gear from the hire shop?'

'Maybe,' he answered, noncommittal. He didn't want to let her know that he'd just gone to the most exclusive shop and bought a whole host of new gear and equipment.

She gave a nod. 'They've obviously improved their range. Cool.'

She gestured towards the ski lift. 'Ready, then?'

'Sure I am. You show me your moves, and I'll show you mine.'

She grinned and glided ahead of him on her skis, lining up with the swiftly approaching chair lift. He slotted in behind her in the queue and tried not to think about how neat her backside had looked as she'd been swept up by the seat. She was wearing the same black ski gear she'd been wearing the first time he'd seen her. And, boy, did it fit well.

They reached the top of the slope around ten minutes later. It wasn't for the faint-hearted, and just being here gave Leo a hint of mischief.

The whole of Mont Coeur lay beneath them, twinkling with lights, surrounded by a dark sky and white snow.

'I love it up here,' Anissa said quietly, her warm breath clouding the air in front of them.

'Impressive,' he said as he looked around. There were only a few other serious skiers. He watched them dart down the slopes in front of them, zig-zagging with ease.

Anissa was moving from foot to foot—obviously anxious to get started. He turned to face her with a wide grin on his face. 'Okay, so you might need to give me a few pointers.'

'What?' Her face fell.

He held up his ski poles. 'You know—the kind of stuff that you teach.'

Her mouth opened. 'But you said you could ski. That you could hold your own.'

He shrugged. 'I might have been a bit economical with the truth.'

Concern laced her brow. 'Please tell me you're joking. I would never have brought you up to this slope if you weren't experienced.'

'I am. I'm maybe just...' he grinned and shrugged again '...a little out of practice.' He loved teasing her. It was clear she was taking it all in and contemplating how to tell him he was about to kill himself skiing down this run.

She sucked in a deep breath and obviously tried to still the panic she was feeling. She shuffled over next to him. 'Okay, let's practise the basics. Positioning. Moving. Slowing and stopping.'

She seemed to go into automatic pilot, demonstrating each position and talking him through it. Leo took great pleasure in getting most things wrong, particularly when she came over and tried to move his body into the position it was supposed to be in.

'When was the last time you skied?' she asked.

'College,' he quipped.

'College?' It came out more like a squeak.

He could see her professional face slip into place. 'Leo, maybe this isn't such a good idea.'

'How long have you been doing this?' he asked. He was curious. Was her dual role between ski instructor and chalet maid her ambition or a convenience?

She bit her bottom lip. It made her look the tiniest bit vulnerable.

'Only for the past year. It's kind of a needs–must situation.'

Now he really was curious. 'Why? What were you doing before?'

She looked distinctly uncomfortable, shifting from ski to ski. 'I had other career plans. But they got…side-lined.'

He couldn't help himself. 'Why, what did you do before?'

She glanced over her shoulder, almost as if she were checking to see if anyone was listening. But the few other skiers up on the slopes were all occupied. She took a deep breath. 'I was a professional. Have been the last few years. I was training for the International Skiing Championship. I was hoping to get gold.'

For the first time since he'd met her, he was struck dumb. 'What?'

She looked a little hurt. 'Is it really so unbelievable?'

'What?' he repeated. 'No, of course not. But…' he paused for a second '…what happened?'

Her face was serious and her body posture tense. 'I had an accident. One that my surgeon termed "catastrophic". I broke my leg in three places. He said it would never be strong enough for me to ski professionally again.'

Leo reached out and touched her arm. 'Oh, Anissa, I'm so sorry.'

She tossed her hair over her shoulder. 'Don't be. I get better every day. I can feel the strength returning. I just need to keep practising, keep conditioning myself to gain momentum again.'

He heard the words she was saying but wasn't quite sure he believed them. He'd seen how much she'd been in shock the other night after her minor accident. And if her doctor had told her that being competitive wasn't possible again, could Anissa be deluding herself?

'What happened to the team you had around you? Didn't you have a sponsor?'

She pressed her lips together and looked off into the distance for a second. 'Yeah. They weren't interested in hanging around. They're in it for the here and now. They don't want to wait for someone to get back to fitness.'

He moved in front of her. It was awkward when they both had skis. Right now he wanted to touch her cheek, give her a hug, let her know that he empathised with her. Because he did.

Anissa sounded as if she'd been the next big thing—only to have it all ripped away from her. In a resort like this, she had a daily reminder of what she'd lost.

He knew how hard that was. He'd spent the last few days purposely avoiding Sebastian and Noemi—even though Noemi had called four times. He was trying so hard to think about the family stuff. He didn't even want to acknowledge how much his life had been turned upside down.

He reached out and took his Anissa's hand. 'I get it,' he said quietly.

Her pale blue eyes met his. 'Get what?' He could see a whole host of mixed emotions there.

'I get what it feels to have your life change completely.'

She narrowed her gaze, a little wrinkle appearing in her brow. 'You do?'

He nodded. He didn't want to say too much. 'Let's just say the reason I came to Mount

Coeur is turning out to be tougher than I originally thought.'

Anissa didn't hesitate. She leaned forward and gave him a hug. He breathed deeply, letting the familiar aroma of her orange blossom scent surround him. He stayed there for a few seconds, enjoying the feeling of her pressed against him.

When she pulled back, he was more than a little sorry. 'Hey,' she said, smiling brightly, 'we came up here to clear our heads and enjoy the view.' She swept her arm out to Mont Coeur beneath them. Nestled in the valley, with mountains and snow surrounding it on all sides, Mont Coeur glistened with yellow lights and exuded warmth. From here it looked like something from one of those Christmas cards adorned with glitter that sat on people's shelves every year.

It gave him a strange pang to realise that he'd never really celebrated Christmas the way he'd always longed to—in an environment where he felt as if he was loved and belonged. Last year's Christmas had been spent in an exclusive restaurant in New York with a visiting work colleague and an annoyed girlfriend. When he'd received the letter from his parents he'd been both excited and nervous about what Christmas might hold this year, all for his hopes to be dashed. It just proved to him he was better off on his own.

He turned to face Anissa again—the brightest spark he'd met since he'd got here. She had her head tilted a little, watching him through enquiring eyes without actually saying anything. It was almost as if she was giving him time for his thoughts. She'd said she came up here to think. He could understand why.

She smiled. 'We're also supposed to enjoy the skiing.' She gave him a sympathetic glance. 'Want to go down to an easier slope? We can do that. You might be more comfortable.' She was being sincere, trying to let him down gently. It seemed he'd fooled her more than he'd planned to.

His stomach gave a little twist. They'd just opened themselves up to each other. Anissa had been going for gold. A gold medal. She'd been *that* good.

And somehow? He wasn't surprised.

He couldn't begin to imagine how much her life had somersaulted. What had happened to her coach? Her team? The sponsors he could almost understand. But the rest?

It made him angry for her. Angry that she was forced to spend her days cleaning other people's chalets and teaching the basics of the thing that had been her passion.

She deserved better.

But she was still thinking about him. She patted his arm. 'It will be fine. Honest. People come up runs all the time that they aren't really equipped to deal with. We'll get you back down and find something safer. Something easier.'

It was the way she was patting his arm. Nicely. Reassuringly. All the while thinking he was probably about to fall on his backside.

Now his wicked streak was beginning to emerge again. He straightened up and looked down the slope. 'How about a little race?'

'What? No.' She was totally surprised. 'This is a run for experienced skiers. I thought you were—but I've obviously overestimated things. It's far too dangerous.'

'You think?' He couldn't help himself, he easily adopted his true skiing position and winked at her over his shoulder as he pushed off.

'Leo!' he heard her shout as he started skimming down the surface of the run. It was fast, glistening in the dark night against the bright white and blue lights adorning the run.

He bent low, picking up speed and bending into the turns. Despite the small lie he'd told Anissa, it had only been a few months since he'd skied and he'd always seemed to have a natural rhythm for it. He loved the feel of the cold air on his face and the speed and freedom of virtually flying down a mountain. Within thirty seconds he heard the swish of skis behind him and heard her calling to him. 'Why, you dirty, rotten...'

He laughed and looked over his shoulder. Sure enough, Anissa was catching up fast, a determined look on her face.

'You lied!' she shouted.

'I was economical with the truth.' The words were lost in the air behind him, but Anissa was there, almost on his shoulder.

'I'll give you a race,' she yelled, bending lower and edging closer.

His competitive edge would normally take over at this point, but inside he was already laughing.

Laughing at the fact he'd fooled her, and laughing at the fact she was determined to win. Anissa Lang played to win. Just another thing to like about her.

There was a flash of black to his right-hand side just as he was about to bank right. He instantly straightened a little, giving Anissa the opportunity she'd obviously planned for as she whizzed past.

He tried to get lower to match her speed. But she was too well in tune with the mountain, too experienced on this slope. She was a natural, moving easily and with ever-increasing speed.

As the bottom of the run loomed ahead his stomach clenched.

'Slow down.' He said the words automatically through gritted teeth. She was still moving at a lightning pace, completely focused, with one intent—to win.

Panic swept over him. But it was as if someone had flicked a switch. All of a sudden she straightened, bending her legs to slow and guiding herself with one pole. It was the most graceful of moves. Perfect. Professional.

He slowed himself, but much sooner than she had. By the time he reached the bottom of the slope she was standing, waiting for him, with a large grin across her face.

She waited until he swept up to join her. She raised one eyebrow. 'Thought you would be a smarty-pants, did you?'

He raised his eyebrows back. 'Now, there's an expression I haven't heard in a hundred years.'

She waved one hand. 'Thought you would fool me?' She put her fingers in the air. 'Let's pretend we can't ski, let's act like a fool, let's see how long it takes her to catch up.'

He opened his mouth in mock surprise. 'Did you catch up? I didn't notice.'

'I chewed you up and spat you out.' She was being snarky but she had a wide smile on her face. 'You wish you could catch me—but you didn't have a chance.' She was taunting him now, obviously picking up on his competitive edge.

He folded his arms. 'I could have caught you.'

She folded hers too. 'Really?'

He nodded. 'I think so. I was being kind. I let you win.'

She pushed down the latch at the back of her boot with her pole and stepped out of one ski. 'Oh, you *let* me win?'

He kept smiling as she pushed down the latch on the other. 'Sure I did. Didn't you know? I'm a gentleman. A gentleman always lets a lady win.'

Now she was free of her skis, Anissa moved around. She crouched down in the snow.

'Who says I'm a lady?' Something flew through the air and smacked him square in the face. For a second he was stunned, choking on the tightly packed snow. Then he spluttered, shook his head and brushed the snow off his jacket. He stepped out of his skis. 'Oh, it's like that, is it?'

She smiled, 'I play to win.' Another snow-ball hit him in the chest and a second flew over his shoulder.

He didn't need to be baited twice. He reached down and grabbed the nearest mound of snow, packing it together and taking aim. Anissa was good. She moved at lightning speed—even in her ski boots. And her hands were even quicker at forming and throwing snowballs.

Pow. Pow. Pow.

'You New York boys,' she yelled. 'Always think you're better at everything!'

'That's fighting talk,' Leo shouted back as he threw snowballs wildly, each one missing the target.

Anissa's laughter rang throughout the night. Leo didn't hesitate. He ran at her, stumbling in his boots. For a second she looked surprised, trying to work out what he was about to do.

But she realised just a fraction of a second too late. Leo yelled as he dived on her, sending her flying onto her back.

*Whoomph!*

Anissa lay flat on her back, looking up at the stars. She was momentarily stunned.

Leo couldn't stop laughing. He had a leg on either side of her and his hands in the snow beside her head.

She blinked, several thick snowflakes landing on her cheeks and lashes. 'You don't play fair,' was all she said.

He kept laughing. 'Play fair? How am I supposed to race a potential gold-medal winner down a slope? Did you tell me before we got up there? Let me know what I was really up against?'

She flicked her head from side to side in the snow. 'I wasn't planning on telling you at all.'

He stopped laughing for a second. She still had a smile on her face. He lowered his face closer to hers. 'I get that. But you were just too cute up there.'

'Cute?' Her eyebrows shot up again, but he knew she wasn't offended, she was still smiling too much.

'We need to stop meeting like this.'

'In the snow?' He nodded in agreement.

She shrugged as she lay there, apparently not minding the fact that the snow was probably soaking through her ski clothes. 'Maybe it was fate? Maybe we were meant to meet?' Her words were light but they struck a strange chord with Leo.

He stopped for a second as he rested back on his legs. 'You believe in fate? After you've been dealt such a harsh blow?'

As he said the words out loud, he realised how much they reflected on his own circumstances. Both of them had had something they'd wanted literally snatched from their fingertips. Trouble was, Anissa had always wanted her goal. Leo hadn't dared to hope, and by the time he'd realised how much he would have liked a relationship with his parents, the chance had gone.

Her answer was quiet. 'I have to believe in something, Leo. There isn't much left.'

His heart squeezed in his chest. Her blonde hair and pale blue eyes were highlighted by the white, white snow behind her head.

He couldn't resist. He bent towards her, brushing his lips against hers. She tasted sweet. She tasted good. And the wave of familiarity from the previous night swept around him.

A tiny part of his brain questioned his actions. What if she objected? But Anissa wrapped her arms around his neck and didn't hesitate when she kissed him back.

Right now, she was all he could think about. And it was a relief. A relief to be wrapped in the arms of a warm, fun, loving woman who he already knew had other issues going on.

It made him feel not quite so alone.

It was crazy. But when Anissa had invited him today for some night-time skiing, he'd known there was no place else he'd rather be. It was odd how two lost souls were being drawn together, both wrestling their demons while trying to get on with their lives.

Her hands threaded around the back of his

head. She pulled her lips from his and whispered in his ear. 'Is this how you plan to win the next race, by distracting me?'

He laughed and whispered in her ear, 'Whatever it takes…'

# CHAPTER FOUR

HER STOMACH WAS in knots. It had been a long time since a guy had made her feel like this. Attractive. Important. Wanted.

She tugged at her top. Black with a criss-cross back, casual but not too casual, paired with jeans. Her hair was down, and she had put on a little more make-up than usual and worn lipstick for the first time in for ever.

Lucy and Chloe sat perched on her sofa, laughing as she frowned at her reflection in the mirror.

She spun around. 'How do I look?'

'Perfect,' said Chloe with a deadpan face as she took a sip of her wine. 'Just like you did ten minutes ago.'

Anissa glanced down. 'Are you sure?' She walked back over to the sofa where a whole array of tops were scattered. 'Maybe I should have gone with the blue? Black's too night-time, isn't it?' She sighed as she turned back to the mirror. 'It's like I'm trying too hard, right?'

Lucy laughed out loud. 'Anissa, you look perfect. Gorgeous. The guy is lucky you agreed to go out with him.' She lifted her glass of wine and raised it towards her. 'And, anyway, it might only be two p.m. out here, but somewhere in the world it's after five.'

Anissa glanced at her glass of untouched wine on the sideboard. The girls had come over to help her get ready. And, of course, they'd brought wine.

She sagged down onto the sofa between them. 'Is it totally pathetic how nervous I am?' She wrung her hands in her lap. 'I'm twenty-eight years, old for goodness' sake. And I feel like I'm thirteen again and going on my first date.'

'You went on your first date at thirteen?' Amy raised her eyebrows and nodded at Chloe. 'Early starter.'

Anissa gave her leg a playful slap and took the wine glass from Amy's hand, stealing a sip.

She put her hand on her stomach. 'What stops nerves?'

'Wine!' said both girls together, laughing.

Chloe nudged her. 'What's to be nervous about? Been there, done that. He's a handsome, rich bachelor who is clearly attracted to you. Just go and have some fun.'

Amy put her hand over Anissa's. 'It's been a crap year, honey. This is your chance to enjoy yourself. To have some fun.' She stopped smiling for a second and squeezed Anissa's hand tightly. 'You deserve this.'

Amy stretched over and lifted Anissa's wine glass, taking it as her own and raising her glass so they all could toast together.

'Here's to late lunches, having fun and some, very, very handsome men.'

'Cheers!' they all shouted as their glasses clinked together.

Leo watched the door. The restaurant was central and popular. He could have easily afforded one of the more exclusive restaurants in the resort but he wanted Anissa to feel comfortable—and this place had been her suggestion.

She strolled in a few minutes late and he breathed a sigh of relief. Nerves were a new thing for him. They'd appeared the moment he'd received the letter from his mother and father and had danced around him ever since.

He'd dated plenty of women in New York for the last few years, even though his priority had always been his business. But none of those dates or eventual brief relationships had resulted in him feeling nervous. He had always been in control. Always polite but slightly distant. Happy to let things progress if they worked out that way, equally happy to let things slide when appropriate.

None of those dates—at any point in the last ten years—had made his stomach churn like this.

It was odd. After the knocks of childhood he'd been so determined to be a confident adult. And he had been—right up until he'd got that letter and the permanent feeling of wondering if he was good enough had made the crows of doubt constantly circle.

So watching Anissa walk through the door towards him was like a breath of fresh air.

She gave him a shy kind of smile as she joined him at the bar.

'Drink?' he asked.

She nodded at his beer bottle. 'I'll have a beer.' He ordered swiftly and they threaded their way through the crowd and found a booth near the back. A waitress appeared promptly with menus. 'Back in five.' She waved.

Leo smiled as he slid into the booth. 'And here was me thinking that everyone came to Mont Coeur to ski.'

Anissa smiled across the crowded bar. 'It's an expensive place to come to stay in a bar all day. Seems like such a waste.'

He looked at her carefully. 'You really love skiing, don't you?'

She sighed. 'It feels like it's in my blood. I can't…not do it. I love it. I love the freedom. The speed. The exhilaration. If I miss it for even one day, I'm itching to get back out there.'

He nodded in appreciation. 'It's great that you've found your passion but—' he chose his next words carefully '—it must have been really tough when you were injured.'

She blinked, and it seemed as though her eyes were wet almost instantly. 'It was.' She swallowed uncomfortably. 'Twelve long weeks. I had to have two separate operations, with six weeks healing in between each. Then I had physio for another twelve weeks.' She gave a wry laugh. 'But I wouldn't stay off the snow. I couldn't.'

'How does your leg feel now? Do you have the strength back?' He was curious but cautious. Would someone really ever recover fully from an injury like that?

She wiggled her leg under the table, brushing it against his. 'Most nights it's still a little sore. Particularly if I've been on the mountain all day. I have to take painkillers. But I was sore every night after training too. So that's nothing really new.'

'But if you don't ski, you don't need the painkillers?' He couldn't hide the concern in his tone.

She gave a shrug. 'I wouldn't know. I never

don't ski.' She said it very matter-of-factly, as if the thought had never occurred to her.

'Do you keep in touch with anyone from before?'

Something flashed across her eyes. A jolt of hurt. She shook her head. 'I'm going to wait until I know I'm back at peak performance before I talk to anyone again. The circuit is small and I'd rather be fully ready before I try to find a new coach.'

He gave a nod. He knew immediately it was about what she wasn't saying. He'd answered enough questions like that himself over the years.

The waitress appeared back at their side. 'Ready to order?'

Anissa smiled. 'I'll have the regular Swiss burger, well done, with everything.'

Leo shook his head. He hadn't even glanced at the menu yet, too caught up in the conversation with Anissa. He handed his menu back with a smile. 'I'll have what she's having.'

'So, didn't you have business to do today?' Anissa leaned her head on one of her hands as she watched him.

He waved one hand. 'Three calls to New York, about a hundred emails, and I have a conference call with Japan later.'

She wrinkled her nose. 'Oh… I meant family business. Isn't that what you're here for?'

He took a breath. Truth was, he wasn't exactly sure what to say. 'I'm kind of in limbo at the moment. I'm just waiting to hear a bit of news before I decide my next step.'

It wasn't untrue. He was still hoping his lawyer would find some magical loophole that would set him free from the terms of the will—even though he'd already been told it was highly unlikely.

He stayed silent for a few seconds as Anissa ran her hand up and down the neck of the bottle. 'What do you do in New York?' she asked. 'A businessman—what is that? It's like a multitude of sins.' She gave a little smile then leaned back in the booth, keeping her eyes fixed on his. 'Maybe you're a serial killer? Or a spy?' She raised her eyebrows. 'Or maybe you're one of those crazy guys who do real estate in New York and star in that reality TV show.'

He couldn't help himself. 'Do I look like a reality TV star to you?'

She ran her eyes up and down his body as if she were really contemplating it.

He laughed. 'Wrong question. I should have asked if I looked like a serial killer.'

Now she laughed too and clinked her bottle

against this. 'Thanks for this, Leo. I needed a little fun.'

He stopped for a second and licked his lips, looking at her appreciatively. 'So did I.' And he meant it. Every word.

This was ridiculous. He couldn't wait to get out of Mont Coeur. He never should have been here in the first place. And it was the last place he'd ever expected to meet someone. But somehow meeting Anissa had made the last few days a bit more bearable. Made the waiting game not quite so difficult.

Christmas was everywhere in Mont Coeur. And for Leo right now it was whipping up a whole range of emotions he didn't quite know how to deal with.

The waitress appeared with their food and set it before them.

Even though it was just early afternoon, the place remained busy and as they chatted the noise levels were rising.

Leo found himself leaning closer and closer across the table to talk to Anissa. She didn't seem to object, mirroring his movements and shifting in her seat until their heads were almost touching. Her hair fell forward and the scent of strawberry shampoo drifted towards him.

From the first time he'd met her he'd been

attracted to her. But the more time he spent around her, the more he seemed to learn. Each encounter made him think that he'd peeled back another layer.

Anissa had qualities he admired. A real edge of determination. The ability to work hard. Drive. But all of these things were partially clouded by a veil of something else— something he strongly suspected was a woman who'd been hurt at some point, and not just by her injury.

It only made him relate to her all the more, and today she seemed more relaxed and at ease around him than she had before.

He was noticing things. Little things. The kind of things that he didn't normally take the trouble to notice. When she chatted she always toyed with the earring in her left lobe. She preferred to tuck her hair behind her right ear. She was observant—and it wasn't that he thought she was bored by him—or at least he hoped she wasn't. But she seemed to love to people-watch, remarking on the things she noticed.

'The girl in the red jacket. Do you think she's on a first date?'

Leo looked to where she was watching, seeing the girl shifting uncomfortably in her chair and sitting stiffly as a guy in a black jacket tried to engage her in conversation.

Leo cringed. 'She doesn't want to be there, does she? Look at that poor guy. He obviously can't stop talking. He looks so nervous.'

Anissa nodded to the right. 'What about the four girls in the booth over there? I sense trouble…'

Leo checked them out and smiled as he sipped the last of his beer. 'I think you could be right. Things look as if they're getting fierce.'

Sure enough, a few seconds later one of them grabbed her bag and jacket and stomped out the front door.

Leo couldn't stop watching Anissa. 'You like this, don't you?'

She finished her beer. 'What? People-watching?' She gave a little shrug. 'Of course. Doesn't everyone? I just usually don't get time. I normally have a shift in the chalets in the morning then I do lessons most afternoons and sometimes into the evenings. It's nice to get a little downtime.'

She gave a wicked kind of smile. 'I sometimes like to imagine whole other lives for people.' She gestured with her head to the couple behind them. 'Those guys? They look normal, but she's actually a princess from some principality and he's her bodyguard. But…' She leaned forward and whispered behind her hand, 'They're actually in love with each other.'

Leo shook his head but couldn't help but smile as Anissa continued. 'And those two over there—at the bar?' She winked. 'They might look like they're just your average couple who just spent the morning skiing, but they're actually time travellers. He's a Roman warrior and she's an Egyptian queen.'

Leo leaned forward conspiratorially. 'You have a very vivid imagination.'

She gave him a naughty nod. 'Oh, believe me, you have *no* idea.'

He liked this. He liked this a lot.

Her phone screen lit up and she leaned forward and smiled, reading the message and tapping out a quick reply.

He couldn't help but ask. 'Who is it?'

'My mum and dad. They're still at home in Austria and they text me every day.' She rolled her eyes. 'Except when we're all watching the latest episode of our favourite sci-fi show at the same time. Then we text every five minutes.'

Her comments were easy and throwaway. She obviously had parents who loved her and supported her. A relationship he hadn't experienced in the past and couldn't develop in the future. The thing that surprised him most was now much that actually gnawed away at him. How much it unexpectedly stung.

The waitress appeared beside them again. 'More drinks?'

Leo reached over and grabbed the cocktail menu. Another drink. Exactly what he needed right now. 'Do you have a preference?' he asked Anissa.

'This early?'

He shrugged, 'It's afternoon. Anyway…' he leaned forward again '…don't we have more people-watching to do?'

She nodded her head, 'I guess we do.' Then leaned her head on her hand. 'So, surprise me.'

His eyes ran down the cocktail list. 'We'll have two of these—the Stormy Slopes.'

The waitress gave a smile, disappeared for a few minutes then returned with two tall glasses.

Anissa leaned over and breathed in. 'Hmm, interesting.' She took a sip through the straw. Almost immediately her eyes sparkled. 'Wow, that's nice. What's in it?'

Leo took a drink from his too and gave a nod of approval. 'Rum, ginger beer and lime. Tasty. Not too heavy.' He gave her a smile. 'Afternoon cocktails. We don't want to fall over. Not yet, anyway.'

She studied him for a second. 'Have you visited any of the shops yet?'

He shook his head. 'Apart from the ski shop?

Not a chance. I've been too busy. I've spent most of my time on the phone to New York.'

'Not much of a holiday,' she reflected.

'It was never meant to be a holiday.' His tone had changed and she looked up sharply and licked her lips but she didn't talk. She didn't try to fill the silence, just ran her fingers up and down the side of her glass.

It was another of her habits. Another thing he'd noticed about her.

He took a deep breath. 'The shops. Are they any good? Anything you'd recommend?'

She gave a little smile, knowing that he was changing the subject. 'Maybe. There's lots of quirky shops in Mont Coeur. Do you have anyone to buy gifts for in New York? I can probably show you where to get something a little different.'

His stomach gave a little flip. This would have been the first year he could actually have bought something for his mother and father. The effect was instant. Underneath his jersey T-shirt his skin prickled. Christmas. The time of year he liked to best avoid. What about Sebastian and his family? What about Noemi? Should he buy gifts for his brother and sister, and what on earth could he buy them? He barely knew them.

The face of his PA floated into his mind.

Keisa had worked for him for the last six years. He usually bought something online and had it delivered. 'I always buy something for my PA.'

'Male or female?'

'Female.'

'What age?'

He wrinkled his brow. 'I thought I wasn't allowed to ask that?' He smiled for a second. 'I think she's probably early fifties.'

Anissa nodded. 'I know a few shops we can go to. You can see if there's anything she'll like.'

They finished their cocktails and wandered out into the snow-covered streets. The light was already beginning to fade. People were bundled up in a variety of coloured parkas, hats and scarves.

Although it was bitterly cold, there was a warmth about Mont Coeur that afternoon. It might have something to do with the fact that this was the first time she'd really been on a proper date in years. Although she knew there was no chance of this going anywhere, no chance of things progressing—his life was in New York as a businessman and hers was here, focusing on her skiing plans for the future—it was nice to be around someone again. It was nice to look at someone and feel as if they were really interested in what you were saying. The electricity in the air between them didn't hurt either.

But she was still curious. He'd mentioned the other night that he was here on family business. But he hadn't mentioned any family he intended to buy Christmas presents for. She hadn't seen anyone else visiting his chalet, so wasn't he close to his family? Mont Coeur was a long way to come from New York if he wasn't particularly close to his family.

They window-shopped along the street, Anissa pointing out a women's fashion store, a traditional Swiss chocolate shop and a jewellery store.

But none of them seemed to capture Leo's attention. Eventually she stopped and folded her arms. 'Okay, what do you normally buy Keisa?' She shook her head. 'Don't tell me. You internet-shop. You buy her perfume. Or some kind of designer scarf.'

Leo's brow furrowed and he turned towards her. 'Have you been spying on me?'

She studied his face and felt a little wave of sadness for him. Why would a guy as nice as Leo only have a PA to buy for at Christmas? It seemed…lonely.

'Why don't you use your imagination? Look at these gorgeous shops. Think about Keisa.

What kind of a person is she? What does she like? Has she ever told you anything that would give a hint of what kind of gift might be a little more thoughtful, a little more personal?'

He gave a slow nod. 'Okay, then. Let's see if I can…' he gave her a wink '…use my imagination.'

As they walked further along the street, his hand brushed against hers. Whilst the little bolt of energy was still shooting up her arm he took her hand in his. She didn't object. In fact, it sent a flash of something through her head.

Her ex hadn't like public displays of affection. He'd never held her hand. He'd never put his arm around her while they'd walked in the street. They'd dated for four years and had practically lived together for the year they'd been engaged. But deep down she wondered if they'd ever really been close.

Everything had been about skiing, about racing. About getting the best times. About coaching. They had never really had many of the traditional 'dates'. Any dinner together had generally been work-related with other ski professionals from different countries. Any visit abroad had always been for a competition or about the sponsors. Just the simple act of taking her hand and Leo had made something pang inside her chest—made her feel as if she'd missed out.

'Wait a minute, what about that place?'

Leo pointed across the street to an old-fashioned shop with tiny squares of window glass outlined in white wood. There was a small Christmas tree front and centre in the window.

Anissa nodded. 'Yes, I'd forgotten about this place. They have lot of wood carvings, Christmas tree decorations, and I think they do some crystal jewellery too.'

Leo pushed open the door and a waft of cinnamon, pine and oranges surrounded them. The whole shop was filled with coloured twinkling lights. They walked around slowly, admiring the carved Christmas scenes, the array of coloured glass pendants and rings, and a whole host of unusual Christmas baubles.

Anissa pointed to a mauve-coloured pendant. 'What about this one?'

Leo bent down to look at the oval-shaped stone. He wrinkled his nose. 'It's nice… I suppose, but…' Then he looked up and his eyes widened. 'Oh, wow.'

Anissa followed his gaze. The back wall of the shop was covered in rows and rows of cuckoo clocks.

Leo stepped over, moving from one to another. Each one was completely individual. Anissa had never really looked closely before at cuckoo clocks, but now she could appreciate the workmanship. She reached a hand up to touch one, hesitating, 'I wonder how many hours one of these takes?'

Leo was moving along the line, studying each one. 'The wooden Christmas scenes,' he murmured. 'Keisa has a whole collection. A whole village. She's told me about them before. A bakery. A school. A Ferris wheel. A skating rink. A church.'

He smiled. 'But she doesn't have one of these.'

She could see the sparkle in his eyes. He turned to face her. 'A cuckoo clock. I know that Austria, Germany and Switzerland all make them. But it's kind of unique.'

Anissa smiled. 'More personal than a bottle of perfume.'

He turned back and kept studying the clocks on the wall, before taking a sharp breath. 'It's this one. It's definitely this one.'

Anissa moved closer to him and looked up. It was a beautiful wooden hand-carved cuckoo clock. Even from underneath, Anissa could see how intricate it was. It was a variety of shades of wood, with some areas carefully painted. There was the traditional cuckoo at the top behind a red door, two little balconies, one with a carved rocking chair, the other with a few birds perched on the edge. Underneath on one side were two children playing on a see-saw, a dog at their side. And on the other side was a Christmas tree with tiny red and blue baubles and a gold twinkling star on top. The whole clock was decorated with a dusting of snow. It really was a work of art.

Anissa felt a tear form in the corner of her eye. 'It's beautiful,' she breathed.

'Anissa.' Leo appeared behind her, putting one hand at her waist and leaning over one shoulder. 'What's wrong?'

She reached up and brushed the tear away, shaking her head. 'It's nothing. I'm just being silly.'

'Silly about what?'

No matter how hard she tried, she couldn't stop her voice from trembling, 'It's just...it looks so perfect. But you can tell the hard work, how painstaking it must have been to create.' She held her hands out in front of it. 'It's like someone's hopes and dreams have materialised right in front of you.' Her mouth felt dry. 'Not everyone gets that lucky.'

Leo's other hand closed around her waist and he pulled her back against him, holding her still. Anissa was very conscious of her chest rising and falling. The wide, supportive feeling at her back.

Leo's warm breath danced across her neck. His voice was low. 'I know what you mean.'

She tensed. She knew Leo was distracted by family issues but she didn't really know what they were. He was a billionaire—at least he must be if he was staying in one of those chalets—so hadn't he already been lucky?

She took a deep breath. 'You said you were here to see your family. Is something wrong? You haven't mentioned them, just that things are...difficult.'

She watched as he swallowed and she saw the deep flash of pain in his eyes. 'I... I guess you could say we're estranged. My brother and sister—it was the first time that we've met.'

'You just met?' He'd already told her he was thirty-eight. Why on earth had it taken that long to meet his siblings?

He gave a slow nod. She could tell he was struggling already with what to say. This wasn't her business. She knew that. And she didn't want to push him to say more than he was ready to.

'Up until a few months ago, Sebastian and Noemi didn't know I existed—or I them. The first meeting was hard. I'm not sure how things will work out. I'm not sure I'm the kind of person to be part of that family.'

There was so much unsaid there. So much visible hurt. Pushing him at this point would be wrong. She turned to face him and reached out and ran her fingers through his hair.

She tried to keep her voice steady as she gave him a sad kind of smile. 'So I guess you don't feel so lucky, then?'

He shook his head. 'Do you?'

She gulped and turned back to look at the beautiful clock. 'Not right now,' she admitted. 'This year has been tough.' She held up her hands. 'Even Mont Coeur, it's the place I need to be, somewhere I can get the chance to practise, but, honestly, for the last year it's felt like a permanent reminder of what I've missed out on, what I *should* have been. What I still want to be.'

His hands slipped around her waist. He didn't say a word, just continued to hold her in his arms. She felt comfortable there. And that was stupid. Because they'd only just met.

She leaned her head back against his chest. She wasn't sure why but it felt safe to talk around Leo. It was even easier to talk when she didn't have to look him in the eye. 'Nothing like getting bad news and turning to your fiancé for support, only to see him move away so quickly he almost wins gold medals himself.'

'That's what happened?' She could feel Leo stiffen behind her.

She nodded her head. 'Yeah. No coach. No fiancé. No wedding. Way to help a girl when she's feeling down.' She was trying to sound ironic but instead she sounded tired and she knew that. But the truth was she *was* tired. Tired of trying so hard all the time on her own.

Leo's lips brushed against her ear as he bent to speak low into her ear. 'Well, one thing is quite clear, the guy didn't deserve you—not for a second.'

His phone buzzed and he moved back. She hated how much she didn't like that.

He spoke quietly. 'Yeah, yeah. Hmm.' He looked at her as she turned around. 'Can you give me a minute?' he said into the phone.

He turned back to her. 'Okay?'

She nodded and tried to pull her thoughts together. 'Should I ask the owner to parcel up the clock while you take your call?'

He nodded. 'That would be great,' he said as he strolled towards the door.

Anissa turned back to the clock. It was beautiful. It was a work of art. A masterpiece. Just like she eventually hoped she could be.

Leo didn't like anything he was hearing. A business deal he'd been working on for the last year had developed a last-minute hitch. 'Why hasn't this been dealt with? He said what?'

Leo groaned. The business associate he was dealing with was an older man. It had taken a good few years to even begin the negotiations.

Joe trusted him. He couldn't leave this to any-one else. He had to deal with these problems himself. He gave a huge sigh, 'Okay, I'll come back. I'll get the first flight.'

He finished the call. New York. He'd wanted to go back there for days. But somehow he knew when he got there, the chances of getting a flight back to Mont Coeur to spend Christ-mas with his new family would get slimmer and slimmer.

Here, he'd had the benefit of a little time. Everything in New York was generally about work, even down to the Christmas charity ball he was obligated to attend. As soon as he re-turned to the States...

He looked back through the window of the shop. Anissa was talking to the store owner as they wrapped the cuckoo clock in tissue paper and bubble wrap. His stomach clenched. The Christmas ball. The place he always took a date.

For the first time, the prospect of consult-ing his little black book suddenly didn't seem so appealing. He felt for his wallet and strolled back into the store to pay for the clock.

'Nearly done.' Anissa smiled as he ap-proached.

'I have to go back to New York.'

Her face fell. 'What?'

His skin prickled. She was upset. He hated

that. He hated that fleeting look of hurt in her eyes. Within seconds she plastered a smile on her face. 'Oh, of course.'

'It's business. A particularly tricky deal.'

Anissa pressed her lips tight together and nodded automatically.

The seed of an idea that had partially formed outside burst into full bloom in his head. He hated that flicker of pain he'd seen in her eyes when she'd talked about being in Mont Coeur and being permanently reminded of what she'd lost. It had seemed so raw.

Maybe, just maybe he could change things for her. Put a little sparkle and hope back into her eyes. Something that he ached to feel in his life too.

'Come with me.' The words flew out of his mouth.

Her eyes widened. 'What?'

He nodded, as it all started to make sense in his head. 'You said you've never really had a proper holiday. Come with me. Come and see New York. You'll love it in winter. I can take you sightseeing.'

Sightseeing. The thing he'd never really got around to in New York.

Anissa's mouth was open. 'But…my job. I have lessons booked. I have chalets to clean.'

He moved closer to her. 'Leave them. See if

someone can cover. If you can only come for a few days—that's fine. But come with me. I have a Christmas ball to attend and I'd love it if you could come with me.' His hands ached to reach for her, but he held himself back. 'I called you Ice Princess before, how do you feel about being Cinderella? Going to the most spectacular Christmas ball in New York? It will take your breath away, I promise.'

Her mouth was still open as her eyes widened. He could almost see her brain processing the invitation. She was considering it. She was actually considering it. And that built a whole host of hopes in his chest that still took him by surprise.

He moved closer. Close enough to drown out the Christmas scents from the shop and to let him just smell her. Anissa.

'Come on, Anissa. Live a little,' he whispered.

He could see her hesitation. See her worries.

But her pale blue eyes met his. There was still a little sparkle there. Still a little hope for him.

Her lips turned upwards. 'Okay,' she whispered back as he bent to kiss her.

# CHAPTER FIVE

'You're going. You're definitely going.'

Anissa stared around her chalet, trying to still the rising panic in her chest.

She'd said yes on a whim. How could she look into those bright blue eyes and say anything else? Particularly when she'd been overwhelmed by emotions.

It was odd how looking at the care and attention to detail in one intricate clock could align itself in her head with someone completing their dream—and leaving her feel so far away from her own.

Chloe and Amy were staring at her expectantly from the sofa.

Anissa shook her head again. 'I can't. I must have been mad to agree. I've got lessons, shifts in the chalets.'

Amy stood up and shook her head. 'We can cover them. Between us. We can cover those shifts. Ore and Anouska will help too.'

Anissa breathed in. 'But the lessons…'

Chloe smiled as she turned her phone around. 'Regan just texted. His dad's better. He's coming back. He can cover your lessons.'

Anissa gasped. Regan was one of the other ski instructors, who'd had to take time off at short notice to go home and visit his sick father.

Chloe nudged her. 'You covered his lessons for more than a week at short notice. I'm sure he'll cover yours. It's time to go on the first proper holiday of your adult life. We're sorted. Now, let's see what we can pack.'

She bent over and scribbled something on a bit of paper. 'Here's my cousin's contact details. She stays in New York. She's at fashion college there. You need anything, or you change your mind about being there—give her a call.'

Amy had already made her way to the cupboard and dragged out a suitcase. 'New York. New York. Here she comes.' She danced about in front of Anissa in excitement, then struck a pose, with one finger on her chin. 'Hmm, what do we think our fair maiden should wear when she's with her handsome billionaire in New York?'

'I have ideas,' piped up Chloe. Anissa laughed. She couldn't believe it. Things were actually coming together. She was going on holiday. She was going to New York.

With Leo.

Her heart gave a little flip-flop.

What on earth did this really mean?

His mind was full. Full of business dealings, full of family dealings, and full of a sense of relief that he was going to get out of Mont Coeur, at least for a few days.

The car he'd sent for Anissa pulled up in front of the private airport terminal. Anissa jumped out, frowning and flicking her head from side to side. 'Where are we?'

He smiled. Today she had on a long bright blue wool coat, a black hat and leather gloves. Her blonde hair framed her face and the colour of the coat was reflected in her pale blue eyes, making them look more intense than ever. She was wearing make-up. Her lips were a little redder than before and her eyelashes longer and thicker.

For a few seconds Leo's feet were frozen to the ground. He'd always thought Anissa was naturally pretty, but today…she was stunning.

She touched his arm. 'Leo? I thought we were going to the regular airport?'

He snapped back to attention and signalled to the driver to get her case. 'No. I have my own plane. Makes things simpler.'

She blinked, then blinked again, as if she

was processing what he'd just told her. 'You have your own plane,' she repeated as he led her up the small detachable stairs and into the comfortable aircraft, nodding a greeting to the steward and stewardess.

There was no waiting. The flight plans had been lodged and cleared, and despite the surrounding snow and temperatures the plane and runway were ready for take-off.

The main part of the plane had large cream leather chairs and glossy wooden tables, complete with entertainment systems. Anissa looked around as if she was waiting to see where she should sit.

Leo waved his hand. 'It's just you and me, you can sit anywhere you please. There's Wi-Fi if you need it. Or, if you want to sleep, there's a bedroom in the back.'

'A bedroom?' Her eyes were wide. She looked at the eight large chairs then turned back to him. 'Leo, just exactly how rich are you?'

He smiled and waited until she'd slipped off her coat and picked a chair then he settled down in the one next to her.

Anissa turned and looked out of the window. 'Anything to eat or drink?' She shook her head. 'No, I'm fine, thank you.'

She seemed a little nervous. 'Once we take

off you can use these buttons to move the seat back and these ones to access the entertainment system.'

She gave a nod of acknowledgment and turned to stare back out the window as the plane started to taxi down the runway.

Leo settled back into his seat and pulled out his two computers. He had multiple things to work on during the flight.

It took Anissa a little time to relax, but eventually she fell asleep for a few hours, waking up when the steward came to ask what they wanted for dinner.

'How long to New York?' she asked when she came back from freshening up.

'Just another few hours. It will be evening there when we arrive.'

She gave a little nod and sat down beside him. He glanced at her entertainment system. She had a popular movie frozen on screen in front of her. The setting? New York at Christmas.

He'd been so engrossed in his work for the last few hours he'd been a poor host.

The truth was he'd asked Anissa to join him on the spur of the moment. Maybe it was wrong but it had made perfect sense in his head at the time. The look on her face had been so sad. Plagued by unhappy memories and feelings of not being good enough. She'd said it out loud.

Someone else fulfilling their dream. And it had made his heart twist in unexpected ways.

Because he completely and utterly got it.

He'd always had that feeling of not being good enough. His adoptive parents had never really been interested in him. It seemed as though the 'idea' of adopting a child hadn't really aligned with the reality of it.

The fact was they'd never really been interested in parenting. They hadn't wanted to go to parents' evenings, school shows or sports events. And it seemed the harder he'd worked the more they'd ignored him.

As he'd got older he'd realised that their resentment ran deep. They'd often mention the business deals they could have done or the opportunities that had slipped through their fingers because they were tied with a child. And they'd never forgotten to add that his own parents hadn't wanted him—now something that he knew wasn't true. It was as if he was supposed to be eternally grateful to them for their sacrifice in taking him.

It hadn't taken him long to realise what a destructive relationship that really was. College life had opened a whole new world for him. He'd worked three jobs so he could enrol at New York College, support himself and study business. He'd never missed an assignment and had been top of his class the whole way through. One of his professors had even spoken to him about one of the business proposals he'd pulled together, giving him the confidence to know that his plans were solid with a real possibility of success.

Most importantly, at college he'd met friends with families who loved them dearly, and had included him in the mix with open, welcoming arms. He'd watched the relationships between fathers and mothers and their sons, none of them similar to his experience at all. It had made him realise how much he'd missed out on. But it hadn't allowed him to shake off the internal sense of not being good enough. The one that had been ingrained in him all his life.

So when he'd recognised that same feeling in Anissa, he'd wanted to do anything he could to help her. He'd watched her on the mountain, knew she was talented. But was she being realistic? Was her dream still truly achievable?

He had doubts. But he couldn't say that to her. Did any potential gold-medal athlete get back to their best after such a severe accident?

She'd been constantly surrounded by the ski life. Had she even sampled the rest of the world? Did she know what other opportunities lay out there?

He'd invited her to New York for partly self-ish reasons. He hadn't really wanted to leave her, and he knew she would be a perfect partner for the ball.

But what could he do for her in return?

He turned towards her as they ate their freshly cooked pasta, prepared on the plane. 'You told me you'd never really had a proper holiday before. Is there anything you'd like to do in New York? Anything you'd like to see, to do or anywhere you'd like to go?'

She pulled back in her seat a little. 'Apart from you, there's only one person in New York I'd like to meet. One of the chalet maids, Chloe, wants me to look up her cousin, Jules. Won't you be busy? You said you had to go back for work and emergency meetings.' She gave a smile. 'Jules is my back-up plan in case you disappear the second we get there.'

He gave a nod of his head. 'I do have work to do. Business is business. But you are my guest. New York comes alive at this time of year. Christmas is huge. There are a million things we can do.'

She looked intrigued. 'Like what?'

He racked his brain. He'd been in New York for years but had never really done any sight-seeing. He was probably the world's worst person to show someone around New York. But there was so much to see and do that he could come up with a standard supply of answers.

'We could walk around Central Park. Visit the museums. Go ice skating. Shop. Then there's the Empire State Building and the Rockefeller Center. Times Square. the Statue of Liberty. I'm sure we can find plenty of things to do to keep you busy.'

'All in a few days?' She looked a little disbelieving. He hadn't really specified how long they'd be here—because he wasn't really sure how long this business would take to conclude.

'Don't forget the charity ball,' he added. 'You'll love it.'

She gave a nervous swallow. 'Yeah, a ball. I'll need to find a ballgown. Might have forgotten to pack one.'

Leo sensed her hesitation. 'Don't worry about that. We can sort that out when we land. Keisa, my PA, will know exactly where to send you.'

She held his gaze for the longest moment, immediately making him think that he'd said the wrong thing.

But eventually she peeled her gaze away and continued with the pasta. 'Sounds good,' she said quietly.

Leo licked his lips. This might be a little tougher than he'd first thought.

As the flight prepared to land, Anissa stared

out of the window, watching the bright lights of New York appear beneath them. He'd always loved this part.

The feeling of coming home.

But this time? It was a little different.

This time he felt unsettled. Where, exactly, was home?

First it had been the plane. Then the mention of the ball. Then the throwaway remark about brushing her off onto his PA.

This had been a bad idea. This was a very bad idea.

But as New York had emerged beneath the smoky clouds she'd felt a tiny spurt of exhilaration. If everything else was a disaster, at least she had a few days in a whole new place. A few days to do things that a normal tourist might do. It could even be fun.

A car had been waiting for them at the airport and after their suitcases had been put in the trunk they'd set off into the city. Leo had squirmed for a few seconds.

'What's wrong?' she asked.

He pulled a face. 'This is going to come out all wrong.'

She shifted uncomfortably. 'Well, whatever it is, just say it.' Had he changed her mind about her being here?

'I forgot to book a hotel for you.' He pulled his phone out of his pocket. 'I'm sorry, I'm so used to being on my own and I was so busy thinking about my business deal that I didn't plan ahead.' He gave his head a little shake. 'In my head it makes sense to stay in my penthouse, but now that we're here… I realise how presumptuous that sounds.'

She understood. She understood completely. They'd already seen each other naked and now he was feeling awkward about where she should sleep.

'We've done everything back to front,' she said quietly as New York flashed past outside.

'I can book you into a hotel,' he said quickly. 'I don't want you to feel uncomfortable.'

'I don't want *you* to feel uncomfortable,' she replied quickly, because the truth was, right up until this second she hadn't thought about any of this. It had just flown off her radar, just like it had his. And now he was mentioning it…well, it was making them both feel uncomfortable.

He sighed, as if he realised just how stilted this all sounded, then turned to face her and put his hand on his chest. 'Anissa, I asked you to join me in New York because I wanted you to join me. But I don't want you to feel any obligation to me whatsoever. This is supposed to be fun. My penthouse is big. I have three separate bedrooms and you're welcome to sleep in any one them—alone. Please don't think that by asking you to come I have any other kind of expectation.' He gestured to the streets flashing past outside. 'Or I can book you into any hotel you choose.' He nodded slowly. 'I'm sorry. I should have thought about this sooner—I guess I'm just so used to being on my own. You decide. Do whatever makes you feel most comfortable.'

She took a few seconds to think then met his gaze. 'Thank you for being so honest. The truth is, as a stranger to a new town, and someone who is not used to travelling alone, I'd probably feel safer staying at your penthouse—as long as you don't mind someone who is most comfortable padding around in thick socks and huge pyjamas.' She gave him a smile. 'Glamour is my middle name.'

'You're sure?'

She nodded, as a feeling of relief spread through her. 'I'm sure.'

He sighed and sagged back against the leather seat. 'Thank goodness. My first guest at the penthouse and I thought I'd just made a big faux pas.'

'I'm your first guest?' Now she really was surprised.

He nodded. 'Sure. I've had other friends

visit over the years, but they've stayed at hotels. Probably because I've been so wrapped up in the business.'

Half an hour later the car slid into an underground parking area and Leo took her to a private elevator.

Seconds later they emerged into a glistening penthouse. It was like something out of a film. The tinted glass windows stretched from floor to ceiling, laying the city out before them. The floor was a dark slate colour and the furnishings cream and glass. It was immaculate—like a place where people didn't actually stay.

And, while it was beautiful, it struck Anissa that there was nothing about this place that said 'Leo' to her.

The kitchen was open-plan, looking into the sitting area with large leather sofas and an extremely expensive-looking dining table and chairs.

She walked over and ran her fingers along the table. 'You get to sit here every morning and eat breakfast looking out over New York City? It's quite a view.'

'It is, isn't it?' He gave a slow nod. 'I should take more time to appreciate it.'

He strolled through to the kitchen and opened one of the glossy white cabinets. 'This is the most important thing.' He waved a package at her. 'Coffee pods. There's a whole variety in there so just pick your favourite.' He stood in front of a fancy machine that probably cost more than she earned in a month, flicking a few switches and pressing a few buttons as he slid one of the pods into place and slotted a latte glass underneath. 'This is all you need to do. Simple. Right?'

She blinked as the liquid frothed into the cup and hid her smile. 'It seems simple,' she agreed. 'But I feel as if I should come with an equipment warning.'

'What do you mean?'

She sighed and waved her hand in front of her stomach. 'It's like I've got an internal magnet. Dishwashers, coffee machines, computers, microwaves all seem to die in my presence.'

He laughed. 'Really?'

She nodded. 'And that's *before* I touch them.' She wagged her finger. 'So, don't say I didn't warn you.'

He glanced at his watch. 'Then let's leave coffee. How about wine? Even your internal magnet can't mess with a bottle opener.' He lifted two wine glasses down from the cupboard. 'What would you prefer, white or red?'

She paused for a second. 'Actually, my favourite is blush. Do you have any?'

He looked amused. 'Hmm, blush. Interesting choice. Yes, give me a minute.'

He pressed a button and a whole wall of the kitchen slid back to reveal a hidden wine rack. Anissa felt her eyes boggle. Really?

He selected a bottle from the rack and turned back, opening it with the corkscrew and pouring a little into one of the glasses. 'Care to check?'

Anissa laughed. 'Honestly? It looks like the right colour, so I'm sure it will be fine.' She rolled her eyes. 'How the other half live, eh?'

She watched as Leo filled both glasses and they walked over and sat down at the table. She looked out at the array of glistening lights.

'So, teach me about New York,' she said.

He gave a nod and pointed, 'That's the Empire State Building, over there is the Rockefeller Center, there's a giant Christmas tree down there and a skating rink we can visit.' He gave her a nod. 'There's also a really cool bakery on the other side of the street.'

'I like how your brain works.' She smiled as she took a sip of her wine.

'Over there, and down a bit, is Times Square. It's more fun at night. I'll take you there and you can climb the stairs and see where the ball drops at New Year.'

'Oh, yes. I'd forgotten about that.'

'There's another Christmas tree at Bryant Park, one at the Met and another at the Natural History Museum.' He looked at her carefully. 'And if you like shopping, there's always Fifth Avenue.'

She gulped. 'I'm not sure I'll be shopping on Fifth Avenue, *window*-shopping maybe. But not actual shopping.'

Leo opened his mouth as if he were about to say something else then quickly closed it again. Thank goodness. The last thing she wanted was for him to offer to meet her shopping bill. Not everyone had his income, and although Anissa had savings, she always worked hard to stay within her own budget.

And shopping on Fifth Avenue was way above her budget.

'What about Central Park?' she asked. 'I imagine it's going to be beautiful at this time of year, all covered in snow.'

He nodded. 'We can do Central Park but beware, it's a lot bigger than some people think. And it will be cold. Very cold.'

'As cold as Mont Coeur?'

Leo nodded. 'On a par. The trouble with New York is that every time we have snow, half the city grinds to a halt. Flights get grounded at the airport and some of the public transport stops working.'

Anissa looked out over the snow-dusted city. 'But surely the snow is no big surprise?'

He shrugged. 'You'd think. But every time there's a heavy snowfall there are problems.'

Anissa stood up and looked out the window. 'I like New York in wintertime. It's pretty.'

He moved next to her, his wine glass still in hand. 'So do I. I guess it's just been a long time since I stopped to notice.'

Nerves were starting to work on her. Either that or it was the combination of jet lag and wine. All of a sudden she was conscious of him standing next to her in his fine knit black jumper and black trousers. Conscious of the rise and fall of his chest. The heat emanating from him. They were side by side but she could see his reflection in the window. In Mont Coeur, Leo Baxter had been handsome. Here? In his own environment, there was something else. An assurance, a confidence that hadn't quite seemed so natural in Mont Coeur. Now he was back on his own turf it seemed to ooze from his pores, drawing her in like some kind of magnet. She almost laughed out loud. Maybe she did have a magnet inside her, and instead of being repelled by another, it was just heightening the attraction.

But her curiosity was sparked. What had hampered Leo's confidence in Mont Coeur?

Was it the family business he'd referred to? He'd told her a little, but she was sure there was more to the story. She hadn't really noticed it to begin with, but now they were here, she could see the difference in his personality.

This apartment was beautiful—a showpiece even. But she was still struck by how little of him there was here. It didn't exactly feel like a home. When she closed her eyes and thought of home her mind went immediately to her mum and dad's house in Austria. Set on a hillside, with old trophies of hers scattered across the shelves, a sofa with two mismatched chairs and a whole array of family photographs, it really was a different place.

She gave herself a mental shake. Each to their own. Who was she judge a billionaire on his apparently impersonal home—particularly when he was letting her stay?

He turned towards her and raised his wine glass. 'How about a toast?'

She smiled and nodded. 'What did you have in mind?'

'To New York. To new beginnings.'

She tilted her head. New beginnings for her or new beginnings for him?

She held up her glass and clinked it against his.

'New beginnings,' she agreed as she turned

and looked back out over the city. Her heart beat a little quicker.

New York. A world of new possibilities.

He strolled through to the kitchen and opened one of the glossy white cabinets.

When she got up the next morning, it was the first time in for ever her leg hadn't ached. She was so used to the feeling, it was strange, but she almost missed it. Her hand reached automatically for the painkillers she normally took first thing in the morning and then she stopped herself. She didn't need them.

Ever since her accident there hadn't been a single day that her leg hadn't ached unbearably.

Maybe it was the extremely comfortable bed? But she wasn't stupid. On average she spent six hours a day on the slopes. Yesterday had been the first time she hadn't.

She showered and pulled on some clothes, fully expecting Leo to have left some kind of note about working today. But, instead, he was sitting at the dining table, finishing a phone call.

He looked up as she walked through. 'I thought you promised me pyjamas and thick socks?'

She shook her head as she looked down at her jeans and simple blue jumper. 'I'm saving

them for later. After a hard day's sightseeing—
what could be more perfect than collapsing into
my pyjamas?' She couldn't take her eyes away
from the view again. Daytime New York and
night-time New York were equally beautiful.

'It's like a window to the world up here,' she
said breathlessly. She pressed her nose against
the glass and looked down. People looked like
ants darting purposely beneath her in a myriad of colours.

She spun back around and leaned against the
glass. 'I thought you had urgent business to attend to. Isn't that why we came back?'

His face was serious for a second. 'Yeah, I've
just spoken to Joe. He's quite the traditionalist.
He wants to meet for dinner.'

'What does that mean?'

'That means that we have the day free to
sightsee.'

Anissa's stomach fluttered. She liked how
that sounded. She liked it a lot. 'So, where to,
then?'

He held out his arms. 'Your wish is my command.'

The first place he took her was an all-American
diner near Central Park that was his favourite
breakfast hangout. It didn't look much on the

outside, but one large stack of pancakes later Anissa was convinced.

He'd been too embarrassed to tell her he had virtually no food in the house—his lone bachelor status meant he rarely prepared meals—and that included breakfast. So he'd dashed off a quick email to his housekeeping services to stock his fridge before they'd left the apartment.

She was wearing that long blue coat again, the one that brought out the colour of her eyes, and he found himself fixating on them.

Next, it made sense to go to Central Park. They tramped through the snow together across the Bow Bridge and down towards the Angels of the Water fountain. Then they wove their way through the park towards Belvedere Castle.

'I never knew there was a castle in Central Park,' said Anissa as they turned towards it.

'It was renovated in the eighties. I think up until then it had been almost neglected. Now it's one of the visitor centres.'

A huge smile broke out on Anissa's face. 'It's perfect, isn't it? Small, but there's something so personal about it.'

'It's been used in some movies.'

'Really?' She spun around and held out her arms. 'Just think, I wonder if a real-live princess ever stayed here.'

Leo was looking at her with an amused ex-

pression on his face. 'I'm not sure that anyone—
royal or otherwise—has ever stayed here.'

'But isn't it nice to imagine?' she said quickly.

New York was sparking something inside
her. Or maybe it was Leo. Or maybe it was just
being away from the thing that had surrounded
her for most of her life—skiing.

'Look at the gorgeous view across the park.'
She turned around and held up her hands. 'Not
that the view from your penthouse isn't magnificent. But this, this is just different.'

His shoulder touched hers as he stood next to
her on the ramparts. 'Don't you get tired of seeing snow all the time? Have you never longed
for a sunny beach and the lapping ocean?'

It wasn't the strangest question in the world
but it kind of took her unawares. 'I've never
had a beach holiday,' she murmured, wondering what it would be like to run about in a bi-
kini all day.

Her hand went automatically to her stomach.
'Imagine having to think about holding your
belly in all day. Or whether you had enough
sunscreen on the places you couldn't reach.'

He gave a small laugh. 'I can assure you, you
don't need to worry about your stomach. As for
the places you can't reach? That's what other
people are for.' His face grew serious. 'Anissa,
how old are you?'

She wrinkled her nose a little. 'Twenty-eight. But I'm sure you're not supposed to ask me that.'

'You really haven't had a proper holiday before, have you?'

Her brain flooded with a whole host of memories. Alain, her ex-fiancé and coach, had always been about the skiing. Always about the lucrative sponsorship deals he could score for her—or, now that she thought about it, for them. Any time they had gone away she'd always been training for the sport and had never had a chance to see the sights. His idea of love had been to push her to be the best skier that she could be.

At the time that had seemed right. But now, standing in Central Park, she wasn't so sure.

She sucked in a deep breath, letting the air come back out slowly, forming steam in the air in front of her.

'Anissa? What's wrong?'

Leo's arm slipped around her body, his arms overlapping hers. 'You're shaking. What is it?'

She couldn't stop the tremble in her voice. 'I'm just remembering things. I'm just realising the number of places I've visited but never actually seen.' She turned around in his arms so that she was facing him. It felt safer this way. Safer than staring out into the expanse of the park.

'I'm just wondering how much I've missed out on.'

She couldn't look into those blue eyes. She didn't want pity. Now she was feeling foolish. Foolish that it had taken her until this moment to see what had been happening in her life. She gave her leg an unconscious rub.

It wasn't sore. It wasn't aching. She'd thought about that this morning. The last time she'd talked about skiing to Leo she'd told him she couldn't bear the thought of not skiing every day. But now she was here—now she had a chance to think about something *other* than skiing—she was wondering how she'd let her life feel so closeted.

Tears formed in her eyes as she tried to swallow the huge lump in her throat. Leo pulled her towards his chest. 'I'm supposed to be making you happy,' he whispered, 'not sad.'

She did something automatic. She hugged back. And it felt good. It felt warm. Even though the temperature around them was zero.

'It's not you, Leo. It's definitely not you.'

He pulled back with his hands on her arms. 'What, then?'

She shook her head. 'I can't explain. But I feel like I'm just waking up.' She gave a wry laugh. 'I'm twenty-eight and I'm just waking up.'

She was embarrassed by how she was feeling. Embarrassed by the whole host of emotions sweeping around her.

Leo tilted her chin up towards him. 'Well, in the spirit of waking up, how about we do something else? What do you say?'

She sucked in another breath to steady herself. 'I say that sounds great.' She pulled her phone from her pocket. 'And I know exactly the place I want to go.'

Five minutes later they had coffee in their hands from one of park vendors and, after a long walk and consulting the map on her phone, she led Leo to an exit halfway up the park.

He laughed when he saw what was ahead. 'You're taking me here?'

She held out her arm. A little buzz of excitement spread through her. 'Where else does any kid want to go but the American Museum of Natural History? Dinosaurs. A giant blue whale. Meteorites. Hours and hours of fun.' She gave another little sigh. 'Childlike distractions. Maybe we both could do with some.'

Leo gave a slow nod of his head. 'I've stayed in New York all these years and I've never managed to get here.' It was almost as if he was talking himself into it. 'One of the guys in the office raves about this place.' He reached out and took her hand. 'Okay. Let's do it.'

* * *

He'd felt a wave of panic earlier when he'd seen how upset she was. But something had told him not to pry—not to press too much. Just to step back and be her friend.

But thinking of Anissa in only friendly terms was a feat in itself. More than once he'd padded through to the kitchen last night and stared at the closed bedroom door, wondering about the woman lying on the other side.

He would never have knocked—no matter how much he'd wanted to.

But even sharing his space with someone else was new to him. No one had slept overnight in the apartment before but him, and it felt different knowing someone else was there. Leo had sometimes prided himself on his own space, his own privacy, and just having her there was an adjustment. It gave him a weird vibe—one that he wasn't quite sure about yet.

Then today, when she'd been standing in front of him in her blue coat, with the snow in Central Park framed behind her, the sight of her had made him catch his breath.

It was odd. Their meeting had been a fluke—entirely coincidental, with a whole set of circumstances they could never have predicted. Who knew he would have been in Mont Coeur at all? His parents dying had been a horrible event. The will reading in Switzerland? He would never have expected that. And for Anissa to be training and have an accident at the exact moment he'd come by...

Then there was the spark. The one that neither of them could deny. And on top of all of that was the fact she'd been sent to clean his chalet.

In another life they would never have met. But they'd met in this one. And it felt strangely right.

Part of this was probably how he was feeling right now. The flood of feelings from childhood and his insecurities had come back with a vengeance. He'd spent most of his adult life determined to shake them off, and for a while he'd thought he had.

Even having that face-to-face conversation with his mother and father would have helped. At least he thought it would have. And that constant sense of being cheated wouldn't leave him.

'Hey, Leo, I've got the tickets.' His head jerked up. Anissa was at the desk, waving the tickets at him.

His hand went automatically to his wallet. 'Oh, sorry, here, let me.'

She shook her head. 'Absolutely not. My treat.' She was smiling with the tickets held up against her cheek. There was a twinkle in her eye—one that had been missing in the park.

He crooked his elbow towards her. 'Okay, Ms Lang, let's have some fun.'

She'd never laughed so much. They'd spent hours in amongst the dinosaur skeletons, wondering at their size and immense power. For a few moments Leo had seemed a bit quiet. 'Always wanted to visit a place like this,' he'd murmured.

'You must have gone to museums with your mum and dad,' she'd said.

'Not often,' was the reply.

But the melancholy moment had left him as soon as it had arrived. If he hadn't been to many museums in his childhood, it seemed he was using this one to make up for it.

Anissa took pictures of them comparing themselves to the huge footprint of the Titanosaurus. Then they wandered through the hall of mammals and the wonders of the ocean exhibit. She couldn't help but gasp at the site of the giant blue whale suspended between two floors.

He nudged her as they looked down onto the floor below. 'Do you know you can stay here? Spend the night?'

'What? No way!' She couldn't hide her excitement at even the thought of it.

'Yep. Guess what's it called?'

Was it a trick question? 'Don't know.'

'"Night at the Museum".'

She let out a burst of laughter. 'After the movie? Oh, I love it!'

He nodded. 'One of the other guys at my work has two kids. When they did it, they got to go around the dinosaur exhibits in the middle of the night with flashlights. He said it was one of the best nights of his life.'

She clasped her hands to her chest. 'Oh, I want to do it. I want to do it.'

He shook his head, smiling. 'Think you have to be between six and thirteen.' He leaned forward and whispered, his lips brushing against her ear, 'I think we might have left it a bit too late.'

She scowled and stood back, looking him up and down. 'Well, you've definitely left it too late. But me?' She held up her hair in pretend bunches and gave him a cheeky smile. 'I could maybe pass for thirteen if I tried really hard.'

He gave her a playful shove. 'No way. If I don't get to hunt dinosaurs at night, neither do you. We could always steal some kids if we have to.'

She nodded her head until a mother walked past with a kid screaming in a stroller. 'Okay,' she whispered, 'just promise me it's not that one.'

She slid her hand into his. 'You know, I did

do this kind of thing with my mum and dad—
just not enough.'

'Why not?' He seemed curious.

She gave a little shrug. 'I was so passionate
about skiing. At times it was the only thing I
wanted to do, and in a way I was lucky because
my mum and dad supported me, but now…'
She stared back up at the giant whale. 'For the
first time I wonder how much I missed out on.
I wonder if at some point they should have said
no to me.'

He turned to stare at her. 'How would you
have felt if they had?'

His bright blue eyes were intense. It was almost as if he already knew the answer. She
gave a laugh and shook her head. 'Oh, I'm sure
I would have been quite the little diva. I didn't
like it when I didn't get my own way.'

He arched one eyebrow. 'You? A diva? No
way.'

She laughed and slid her arm into his.

Next, they spent time in the human and cul-
ture halls before heading to the planetarium.

'I love this,' breathed Anissa, as she lay back
in one of the tilting chairs and looked at dark
universe above scattered with stars. Music was
playing around them as the show continued.

'It is pretty amazing,' agreed Leo as he lay
in the chair next to her. She turned her head.

He was staring straight up, his dark, slightly messy hair crinkling at the collar of his button-down shirt. Most men had their hair cropped quite short, but she liked the longer look. It suited Leo. And every time she looked at that hair she had to fight the urge to run her fingers through it.

There was hardly anyone around them and for a few moments it felt as if they were only ones appreciating the marvels above them.

She reached over and threaded her fingers through his. If he was surprised he didn't show it. He didn't pull away. 'Thank you for bringing me here, Leo,' she whispered.

He turned his head in the darkness and smiled at her, just as the planets appeared behind him. 'I think you brought me,' he joked as she let out a gasp.

It was odd. She'd seen lots of wonderful things today, and snapped a hundred photos. But this was image that would stay in her mind. Leo, lying back in the chair, smiling at her with the planets behind him.

He glanced behind him and nodded at the scene. Settling back in his chair, his thumb traced little circles in the palm of her hand as the show continued. 'I wish I'd done this as a kid,' he murmured. She could see him glanc-

ing at the few other people—many families—
in the theatre.

'You must have done some stuff like this as
a kid?'

He shook his head. 'No. Never. No parks. No
museums. No arcades.' He gave a sad kind of
smile. 'Obviously, I did school trips—and we
went to some fun places then.'

Her stomach rolled. It was almost like he was
trying to make excuses for his parents. What
kind of people had they been? It made her heart
pang. 'Not all families get time,' she said, trying to be conciliatory.

He gave a sad sigh as he continued to trace
little circles in her palm. 'Even if they'd had the
time, they still wouldn't have brought me here.'
He turned to face her. 'But it doesn't matter
now. Because I'm here with the right person.'

Tingles shot up her arm and straight to her
heart.

It was crazy. She knew it was crazy. They'd
done everything back to front. Her actions
that first night had been so out of character for
her she hadn't even recognised herself. She'd
thought she'd have been filled with a lifetime
of regrets.

But…something, something had just clicked.

If someone had told her this time a few
weeks ago she'd be in New York, staying in a

billionaire's penthouse, she would never have believed it.

She wanted to ask him what he meant about the fact his parents still wouldn't have brought him here. And she still hadn't really worked out why he'd only just met his brother and sister. His whole family dynamics seemed complicated and it was obvious he played his cards close to his chest. But now didn't seem the time to ask. Not when he'd just told her he was glad he was with her.

She turned back to him and smiled again, hoping to distract him from any sad thoughts he might be having.

'I wonder if there's anything out there?' she said.

'Who knows?' asked Leo. 'And what do you think they'd make of us?'

Her head fell back, 'Well, that's the million-dollar question, isn't it? We have all this beauty and we've ruined some of it.'

He nodded in agreement, his finger still moving soothingly in her palm. 'You're right. But for now let's just lie back, appreciate the stars and try to imagine a place where everything is perfect.'

There was something about his words. It was like a warm blanket being snuggled all around her. There were a hundred things she could stress about right now. Training. Her job. Her finances. And whether she would ever have a chance of competing professionally again. Sometimes it made her brain ache.

Today had been her first day of a proper holiday. And she'd loved every minute. Or almost every minute. Right up until she'd realised what her life before had been like.

It was almost as if a fog was being lifted from her eyes and she was finally getting clear vision. And the person clearly in her vision right now was Leo.

She smiled again and settled back in her chair. Above her the planets were aligning with stars, sending beautiful streaks across the sky.

It was almost like a message. A message that she was going to take some time to consider. And she knew just who to do that with.

# CHAPTER SIX

LEO HAD ALWAYS been familiar with the tourist spots in New York but he'd never really visited them.

The time at the Natural History Museum had tugged at something inside. In one way, he'd felt a wave of anxiety when he'd seen the tears in Anissa's eyes at Belvedere Castle. It had pulled at all his primal instincts to protect her, and try and take away the hurt she was experiencing. The museum had been the nearest place to go that might distract her.

But it had done a whole lot more than that. She'd come alive in there. He'd almost felt her confidence build as they'd moved around the museum. He'd loved watching the excitement in her eyes at some of the exhibits. She could find joy in the smallest things, and had a million ideas, opinions and questions—all things he'd never really thought about before.

Being around Anissa was fun. The truth was

at Mont Coeur there had been an air of sadness around her—even if she hadn't known it. He knew it was likely due to her uncertainty and her change of circumstances, but the more hours she spent in New York, the more he could see her gradually shaking off those worries and feelings. And he liked that. He liked that a lot.

Because she was having an effect on him. Today he'd sent a text to Noemi. It was ridiculous. It had taken him nearly an hour to decide what to send.

Hi there, had to return to New York for urgent business but will be in touch soon. Won't do anything to jeopardise Cattaneo Jewels.

He'd wanted to be reassuring. Noemi had replied straight away, saying that she hoped everything was okay.

He'd felt a little bad that he hadn't spoken to them before he'd left. But he wasn't used to this family stuff. He wasn't used to keeping in touch with people.

Watching Anissa send frequent texts to her mum and dad had made him feel guilty.

He really needed a chance to try and get his head around all this.

But now wasn't the time. Because right now he was steering Anissa along Fifth Avenue.

She stopped outside one store then another. He watched closely. He could see when something caught her eye. 'Want to go in?'

She shook her head. 'Not a chance. I'm a window shopper. That's it.'

He tried to be tactful. 'Well, one of things I wanted to take you to was the Christmas ball. It's fancy. You'll need something formal. And obviously it's my treat. So if you see something you like and want to try, go ahead.'

She hesitated for a second, apparently struggling to find the words. 'Leo... I'm really honoured you want to take me somewhere like that...and I'd never want to embarrass you, but I'm not quite sure how comfortable I feel about you buying me something that...' She held out her hand and gestured to the store behind her. 'That will probably cost more than I earn in a few months.'

He'd somehow known Anissa might feel like this. 'But it's my treat. I want you to buy something. Something you like and feel comfortable in.'

She pressed her lips together. 'Let me think about it. I'm just not sure.'

He nodded his head. He had to respect her

wishes. 'Of course. But don't leave it too late. We only have another three days until the ball.'

She glanced along the street. 'Enough of Fifth Avenue. Let's have some fun.'

'What kind of fun?'

She pulled something from her pocket. 'I have a list. I made it last night.'

He sidled up to her and tried to look over her shoulder. 'You made a list?'

She whipped it away so he couldn't see it as she laughed. 'Yep, I wrote down all the things I could possibly do in New York.'

She pulled out her phone and stared at it as it buzzed. The weirdest expression flashed over her face.

'Who is it?'

She gave a little shake of her head. 'It's someone I used to deal with.'

'Your coach—your ex?' He couldn't help it. It was first person that sprang to mind. It didn't matter he'd never set eyes on the guy, there was a definite flicker of jealousy.

She shook her head harder as she still stared at the buzzing phone. 'No, no. It's someone who worked on the championship skiing committee.' She genuinely looked puzzled. 'I have no idea why they want to speak to me.' She pressed her lips together and hit the reject button, sending the caller to her voicemail.

'You don't want to speak to them?'

'No. Not now. Not here.' She still had the list in her other hand. She waited for a second then put a smile back on her face. 'This is about us. This is about New York.'

He wanted to ask more questions. But it was clear she was trying her best to put Mount Coeur behind her. 'Okay, then, what's next on the list?'

She concentrated hard for a few seconds, laughing as he kept trying to duck behind her to see the list.

'Okay,' she said, tucking the list back into her pocket. 'I'd really like it if we could see the view, either from the Empire State Building or the Rockefeller Center—whichever you think is best.'

'I think this is my time to cringe,' he admitted.

'Why?'

He pulled a face. 'I've never managed to get up either, but...'

'How long have you actually lived here?'

He gave a rueful shake of his head. 'No. I think I'm going to take the first amendment here. I don't want to implicate myself at all.'

She held out her hands. 'Well, just think. We get to do a first thing together.'

He couldn't help but be surprised. And a little impressed. 'Yeah, that's a cool way to look at it. In fact—' Another thought sprang into his head. 'There's actually something else that would be a first—that we can do together.' He gave a slow nod. 'Actually, it makes it easier for me to decide which place we go to for the view.'

He held out his hand towards her. 'Want to see a little more of New York?'

She shot him a huge smile. 'Absolutely.'

The tree was stunning. She'd never quite seen anything like it before. It was around seventy feet tall and stood right in front of the Rockefeller Center, overlooking the most perfect ice rink.

He leaned over the barrier alongside her. 'If we stay here for another week we could see the Christmas tree-lighting. They do it live on television now. It's a big deal.'

She sighed. 'Oh, that would be great. But we'll be back in Mont Coeur by then, won't we?'

There was an almost wistful tone to her voice. Didn't she want to go back to the place she was currently calling home?

Mont Coeur. It was odd. But the name made it feel as though a dark cloak had settled around his shoulders. So much uncertainty. So much still to sort out. He wasn't quite sure if was ready for all this.

'Probably,' he said finally.

She was watching the people skating underneath them. Some were clinging onto the barrier at the side, others were stumbling around the rink and a few were spinning around and skating backwards with ease.

'Want to go skating too?' he asked.

She pointed at one girl who was twirling around in the middle of the rink. 'Just so you know, that's not going to be me, not even close.'

He pointed to a guy who was trying to gain his feet at the side of the rink—and failing miserably. 'Is that going to be you?'

She laughed. 'Let's just wait and see.'

She looked upwards. It was afternoon and the sky was beginning to darken above them. 'Are we going to up?'

He nodded. 'Let's go. This is the perfect time. You'll get to see the city at the end of the daylight, then you'll get to see it in the dark too.'

They made their way inside and he bought the tickets and they boarded the elevator. By the time they exited above the viewing platform sixty-eight floors above, the sun was just starting to descend in the sky.

Anissa couldn't believe the view. There was a glass wall straight in front of them. 'You can walk right around?'

Leo nodded. 'There's a three-hundred-and-sixty-degree view up here.'

She walked over to a set of binoculars and fumbled in her pocket for some change. Leo was quicker and slid some coins in while she still trying to make sense of the American currency.

'The Empire State Building is amazing,' she breathed as she peered through the binoculars. 'The rest of midtown is just amazing.'

'Is that your favourite word today?'

She looked up from the binoculars. 'It could be, but let's wait until we've done the skating.'

They moved around all sides of the viewing platform, spending time looking over Central Park and then east towards Brooklyn.

She gave an appreciative nod. 'The view from your apartment is good, but this, this is just...'

'Amazing?' he finished with a laugh.

'Yeah,' she agreed. It was over an hour before Anissa finally decided she was done. By then, she'd worked her way back around to the south view in time to see the Empire State Building light up.

'It changes colour all the time,' said Leo. 'Traditional is white, but if there's a big sporting event, a special day or support for a charity, or a past historical event then the colours change.' He gave a smile. 'Then, of course, there's Christmas. It usually lights up in red and green just a few days before.'

She gave a rueful kind of smile as she stared over at the Empire State Building currently illuminated in white, her head rested on his shoulder. 'We'll miss that. We'll be back in Mont Coeur.'

His hand slid around her waist and it seemed only natural to turn around to face him. 'Thank you for bringing me to New York, Leo,' she whispered, her warm breath steaming in the cold air around them. With his Italian good looks and sincere eyes he almost took her breath away. For a few moments, even though there were people around them, it felt like it was just the two of them—no one else.

For a second she wondered what he might do, then his head lowered towards hers, his eyelashes brushing against the skin on her cheeks as his lips met hers.

She slid her arms up around his neck. She couldn't think about anything else. Just his lips on hers. She could feel all the tension she hadn't even realised was there melt from her body as Leo deepened their kiss and pulled her even closer. His hand slid down to her backside and the spark she'd felt that first night flooded through her again, coupled with the connection she'd felt today when they'd lain in the planetarium, watching the night sky above them, with their fingers entwined. Leo Baxter was getting well and truly under her skin.

They broke apart naturally, both trying to catch their breath. She let out a little laugh and stepped back as she saw a few other people staring at them.

He stepped back too, with a nod of his head.

He gave her a nudge. 'How about a visit to a bakery in the next street, then we can try the skating?'

Her stomach gave an automatic rumble and they both laughed. 'Well, okay, then,' she said.

The elevator ride down was swift and the white-trimmed popular bakery was right around the corner with a queue out the door. One of the servers gave Leo a wave.

'You know them in here?' Anissa asked, her eyebrows raised.

'Perhaps.' He shrugged. 'Have a look in the counter. They have cupcakes, scones, desserts, pies, cheesecakes, speciality cakes.' He pointed to one end of the counter. 'They even do a speciality cupcake every day.' He squinted around the guy in front of him. 'Today's is banana, pineapple and pecan with cream-cheese icing.'

She groaned. The smell in the bakery was wonderful and was making her hungrier by the second. The queue shuffled slowly forward. 'Okay,' she asked. 'What would you recommend? Somehow I think you might have tried a few of these.'

'Guilty.' He gave a grin. 'Honestly? It would have to be the banana pudding.'

She was kind of intrigued. 'What's in that?'

'Vanilla wafers, fresh bananas and creamy vanilla pudding all topped with chocolate shavings. Once tried, never forgotten. I promise you.'

Her stomach rumbled again. 'Okay. I'll go with that.'

Two minutes later they had piping-hot coffee and small tubs with spoons. It was growing even darker outside with the cold air starting to bite. 'Oh, this is perfect,' Anissa said after the first mouthful.

Leo was watching her anxiously. 'Glad you didn't fold and get a cupcake or a brownie?'

She took another spoonful and shook her head. 'Not a chance.' She glanced over her shoulder. 'But when does it close? We should have bought some cupcakes for the penthouse.'

'Don't worry. They deliver,' he said as they walked back towards the skating rink.

The lights were on around the rink now and it was busier than before. They stood for a minute, finishing their coffee and pudding, before Leo headed over to the skate hire. A few minutes later he came back with two sets of blue skates. Anissa quickly laced hers and stood up, wobbling, while Leo handed over their boots. 'Who is the gold statue?' she asked.

The giant statue overlooked the rink in front of the Rockefeller Center. 'It's Prometheus, and it's made of bronze. I think it's supposed to depict him bringing fire to mankind.' It glistened against the dark night sky, surrounded by the colourful flags of many nations and twinkling lights in the trees around the sunken plaza. 'This whole place is just magical,' breathed Anissa as she tucked her hands back into her gloves.

Leo was waiting for her at the entrance to the rink. He held his hand out towards her. 'Ready?'

She took a few precarious steps towards him. 'Oh, I'm ready. Let's go for it.'

His bravado lasted around five seconds. Long enough to realise he should have held onto the edge.

Anissa stared open-mouthed as he landed flat on his back. Then she couldn't help pull him back up for laughing. People moved past them, a few shuffling, others moving gracefully.

'Hey!' shouted Anissa as he grabbed onto her

legs to finally balance himself. A few seconds later he was facing her, breathing hard. 'Right. Let's try this again.'

She burst out laughing once more. 'Whose idea was this?' she asked as she spun away and did a wobbly kind of twirl.

'Hey, cheater. You said you didn't know how to skate!'

She shook her head as she glided back towards him. 'No. I didn't.' She gave a wicked grin. 'I might have hinted that I wasn't very good.' She gave his chest a prod. 'Just like someone else did on the slopes. Are you trying to play me again?'

He put his hands down to her waist, anchoring her next to him. 'Oh, I promise you. I'm definitely not trying to play you. This seemed like a good idea at the time—but I might live to regret it.'

'What's a few bumps and bruises between friends?' Her eyes were twinkling underneath her blue hat and her cheeks had a glow about them, lighting up her normally pale skin.

A warm feeling spread through him. She was blossoming. She was blossoming in New York, being here with him. What must it have been like, spending most of her life concentrating on training? Had she ever really had time for herself or for friends?

Maybe she'd just needed the break—the freedom to get away and try and find out who she was, what she really wanted to do. Back in Mont Coeur she'd seemed so determined, so focused.

He took a deep breath. 'Have you thought about what you might do if it the skiing thing doesn't work out?'

He could see her whole body tense. Her jaw clenched. 'Why would my…' she lifted her fingers '…"skiing thing" not work out?'

Wow. She was instantly mad. Interesting. He thought carefully. He could skirt around the edges but he got the distinct impression that might be what everyone else did. 'You've had a horrible injury.' He gestured down towards her leg. 'And you've been lucky.' He could see her jaw tense even more and sensed she wanted to butt in, but he was determined to keep talking. 'You've had surgery. Rehab. And you've got your mobility back. You're up, about and walking, with very few problems.' He licked his lips. 'There might be a chance you won't quite reach where you were before. What will you do then?'

For a few seconds it looked as if he'd swept the feet out from under her. She blinked a few times and her eyes looked glassy. He was determined not to fill the silence. After a few minutes she licked her lips and spoke carefully. 'Maybe I am lucky—I guess it's just not really a word that I thought applied to me. You're right. There are other sportspeople who've had horrible career-ending injuries and never got…' this time when she put her fingers in the air she didn't seem mad '"back to normal" like I have.' She sucked in a long breath. 'But my normal was a woman who had the chance of winning championship gold. I'd feel like a quitter if I didn't try to get back to where I was before.'

His hand moved and rubbed her back in reassurance. 'I know, I think it's great. But you've got to have a back-up plan. Even when I throw everything into a business deal, I always have a back-up plan. It's sensible.'

He was trying his best to ask the question without being quite so blunt.

She attempted a smile. 'A back-up plan. I guess it is the sensible option. The grown-up option. I guess I need to look at other things too.' She rolled her eyes and pointed at the ice rink. 'So, Leo, what's your back-up plan for this?'

Now he rolled his eyes too. 'I might need to fake an injury.'

She shook her head and laughed. 'Oh, no. Come on,' she said, obviously taking pity on him and sliding her hand into his. 'You just keep your feet still and I'll pull you round.'

He could tell she wanted to change the subject and move onto something else and that was fine. He'd asked the question and it was clear it was something she'd need to consider. Right now, he had more immediate problems. He couldn't help but look down at the glistening ice, trying to focus on keeping his balance as she tugged him along. The first time he looked up, he started to wobble and Anissa skated around behind him and put her hands at his waist. 'Here, this might be easier. I'll help you keep your balance, and you try and move your feet.'

He tried a few steps, still wobbling furiously. But her hands were steady, and after a few minutes he started to get a little more confident.

Leo almost laughed out loud as a kid stumbled past with his mother holding onto his waist the same way Anissa was. It made him straighten up a little. He could see other people around him struggling too. He bent his knees a bit more and tried to push himself along a little better, trying to glide. His arms were held out on either side as he fought to keep his balance. Anissa leaned around from behind him, her blonde hair coming loose from her hat. 'That's better. You're getting it. Keep going.'

And he was. Little by little he made his way through the rest of the jostling skaters. After a few circuits of the busy ice rink, Anissa released her grip on his waist and appeared back at his side, slipping her hand into his. They looked like any other couple at the rink, laughing and joking on their way around.

He'd never done this before. Never. In fact, there were a number of firsts he'd had in the last few days—all with Anissa. The truth was he'd come back to sort out work issues and he should have been concentrating on convincing Joe to go through with the deal. But Joe was being stubborn, just as Leo had known he would be. He'd agreed to dinner, but not until tomorrow night. Under any other set of circumstances Leo would have been anxious. He'd have been planning ways to either charm Joe or convince him with facts and figures. Whichever strategy worked best. But he hadn't done any of that. He'd been too busy entertaining Anissa.

By the time she tugged him towards the exit of the rink, both of them were breathing a little faster. 'That was fun,' she said.

He let out a wry laugh. 'Yeah, fun.' Then he stopped for a second. 'Actually, it was…better than I thought it would be.'

She leaned on the barrier. There was a distinct gleam in her eye. 'You thought you'd be better, didn't you? You thought you'd just go on out there and ace it.'

She was spot on. He ducked down to unfasten his skates so she wouldn't notice the flush of colour in his face.

But Anissa was just as quick. She knelt down next to him. 'Yes, Leo Baxter. Mr Wonderful at Everything.'

She was joking—of course she was—but the words made his stomach twist.

For a split second their gazes connected and the words just spilled from his lips. 'If only that were true.' He couldn't hide his bitterness.

Her eyes widened and her hand reached over and gripped his jacket. 'Leo?'

He pulled away, embarrassed that he'd let her see his old resentment bubbling over. She fumbled to pull off her skates and quickly changed into her boots. He could see her hesitation as she reached towards him again. It was busy at the changing station. Lots of people were queuing to hire skates. But when her warm hand came into contact with his face he couldn't deny the buzz.

It didn't matter that it was busy. It didn't matter that the level of noise around them was distracting. All he was conscious of was her touch on his face.

She stepped right up to him, her body in full contact with his. It was almost as if a bubble formed around them. A quiet descended, letting the world outside dissipate. Now he couldn't hear the people chattering, now he wasn't conscious of the flashes of colour as people pushed past. All he could see was the pale blue eyes looking up at him.

Her hand was still on his cheek. 'Tell me, Leo. Tell me what's wrong.'

His first reaction would always be to brush things off. To walk away. To change the conversation to something else entirely.

But, somehow, with Anissa, he didn't feel as if he could do that.

His chest grew tight. The weight of his mother and father's deaths. The strained relationship with his new siblings. The pressure of the will.

How could he explain any of that in a few words? He didn't even know where to start. Leo had never had a confidante. Never really disclosed any of his past to friends or colleagues.

He was the original child who kept things close to his chest, and he'd carried that trait into adulthood. No one could protect him or look after him as well as he could look after himself. He'd just believed that for so long.

It had affected everything. Every relationship he'd formed. Whether that had been work or personal. He'd never dated for more than six months. After that, women had expectations about what they thought should happen next. That didn't work for Leo. He hadn't wanted to play the doting husband or father.

He'd never seen that relationship. He'd never had that example.

And now? He never would.

The pain struck him like a crushing blow to the chest. He bent over, trying to suck some air into his chest.

'Leo? Leo? What's wrong? Are you sick?'

Anissa's arm was around him instantly, her head down next to his.

In his mind right now all he could see was the funeral. Of course, he had gone. It hadn't mattered that he'd never met his brother or sister.

Because Salvo and Nicole had been so well known for their business the chapel had been packed. No one had noticed one more Italian-looking man slipping in wearing a black suit. When the family had entered Noemi had been openly weeping, Sebastian's face like a mask.

The two caskets had been side by side at the front of the chapel, a simple white wreath on top of each one.

The congregation had sung a song that his mother had apparently loved—something Leo had never learned. The priest had spoken at length about their lives and love for each other. And their family. Sebastian and Noemi. It had been like a knife twisting in his gut. Leo, the unknown and forgotten child.

He wasn't quite sure what he'd expected to get from the funeral. Essentially he'd been saying goodbye to the parents he'd never got to meet. There had only been a few telephone calls. And for the shortest time he'd felt hope… hope that the one thing he'd always longed for might finally be within his reach—only to have it snatched away from his grasp so cruelly.

It played on his mind, along with the permanent feeling of never being good enough—the one his adoptive parents had continually perpetuated. Even now, Sebastian had resurrected those feelings by his reaction to the will's decree. His face and demeanour at the idea of Leo being involved in the family business had said it all.

It still made him angry. Sebastian had no idea how hard Leo had worked, or just how successful he was. Penthouses in New York and private jets didn't come cheap. Or maybe he did know—and just didn't care.

It turned around in Leo's head. How would he feel if someone came right now and told him he had to share the controlling interests in his business with other people? He'd be angry. He'd be furious. Just like Sebastian clearly was.

Leo's brain was in overdrive. He'd been trying so hard not to overthink everything. He'd been trying so hard just to let himself be distracted for a few days.

Anissa.

It was as if that quiet bubble around him vanished. Anissa's orange scent drifted around him, and the noise from the ice rink and bright lights seemed exaggerated.

Wonderful—that's what she'd said. Leo Baxter wasn't wonderful. Even though he'd tried to be at various points in his life. He wasn't wonderful at being a son, a brother, or at any kind of relationship. Wonderful was the last thing he felt. Especially while all this was going on.

Her hand was at his side. He could see the worried expression on her face and the concern in her eyes. But all of a sudden he didn't want to know.

He needed some space.

He stepped out of her reach. 'I need to go. Is there somewhere else you wanted to see? You mentioned you had a friend to catch up with.'

'Leo?' She blinked then added quickly, 'Of course. Jules. I can give her a call and see if she's available.'

He knew he sounded detached. 'Good. I have

business to deal with.' He grabbed his wallet from his jacket pocket and pulled out a couple of cards. 'Here. Use this for the cab—or for coffee, or drinks—whatever you need.' It was almost as if something flicked on in his head. 'Or if you have time go shopping with Jules, get a dress for the ball.'

He turned and walked away before she had a chance to say anything.

Before she had a chance stop him.

And he walked. Pushed his way through the Christmas crowds and as far away from the merriment that he possibly could.

Anissa was stung. What had just happened? What had she said? She stared down at the cards in her hand. One was a credit card, the other the entrance key to the penthouse.

Someone jostled her from behind and she almost dropped them. 'Get a dress,' he'd said. Did he really think she would just go and spend his money?

She wanted to run after him. She wanted to find out what on earth was wrong—what on earth she'd said.

But something told her not to. Something told her he needed time on his own. She still hadn't really got to the bottom of what was happening in Leo Baxter's life.

She moved away from the ice rink. The joy and excitement she'd experienced earlier deflated—just as if someone had pricked her with a pin.

Her feet carried her back to the bakery. She stared at the card in her hand. There was a tiny flare of anger. He had no idea what kind of person she was. She glanced at the designer store across the road. She'd never been a fan, but she could go in there and come out with a bag, shoes, jeans and coat that would easily total around ten thousand dollars.

For a few seconds she actually contemplated it, staring down at her worn black boots. There was a mannequin in the window dressed in cream coat, black shiny boots and a gold bag. But what use would a cream coat be anyway? She'd get it dirty within the first five minutes.

She sighed and joined the queue in the bakery again, ordering twenty-four cupcakes to be delivered to the penthouse. Her hand wavered as she gave the server Leo's card, wondering if she should just pay for them herself.

But the server moved at lightning speed, handing the card back and packaging up the variety of cupcakes in a cardboard box.

Anissa started walking slowly back down the streets. Maybe she should take a chance and call Jules, even though she didn't really know her. Her hand fumbled in her pocket, rustling a scrap of paper as she tucked the cards inside. She stopped and pulled it out.

The contact details Chloe had given her for her cousin. She swallowed and looked around. She didn't want to go back to the penthouse yet—not if Leo was there. And she didn't really want to wander around alone. Maybe Chloe's cousin could tell her somewhere fun to go for a few hours—somewhere safe, and hopefully warm. She pulled out her phone and started dialling.

One hour and one subway ride later, Anissa was on her second bottle of beer with Chloe's cousin, Jules.

Jules had been happy to hear from Anissa and invited her to join her and her friends in a local bar. Jules was dressed in a variety of black clothing with her thick dark hair swept over to one side. Her fingers picked at the foil around the neck of the bottle of beer. 'So you're telling me that some billionaire gave you his credit card, told you to spend, and you didn't do it?'

Jules was looking at Anissa as if she were entirely crazy.

'I bought cupcakes.' She shrugged.

Jules shook her head. 'Cupcakes.' She reached across the table and grabbed Anissa's hand. 'Girl, you're in New York. You could have bought just about anything! A pair of Louboutins. A Louis Vuitton bag. And you bought cupcakes?'

Anissa sighed and leaned her head on one hand.

'Your guy sounds like a bit of a tool,' remarked Jules.

'He's not my guy.'

'Then what is he?'

Anissa shifted uncomfortably on her bar stool. She wasn't quite sure what to call Leo. 'He's just…just…a friend.'

Jules eyebrows shot up. 'A friend? But not your guy.' She counted off on one hand. 'So, he flies you to New York in his private jet, installs you in his penthouse with no strings. Takes you sightseeing and ice skating. Invites you to some party. Kisses you at the top of the Rockefeller Center, then abandons you at the ice rink and stomps off in a huff somewhere.'

Anissa rolled her eyes. 'When you put it like that…' She sighed. 'And it's not a party. It's a ball. He told me to buy a dress.'

Jules sat a little straighter on her stool. 'Ball? What ball?'

Anissa waved her hand. 'I don't know. Some Christmas charity ball. It's in that famous hotel on Fifth Avenue, next to Central Park.'

Jules's chin almost bounced off the bar. 'Wh-what?'

Anissa felt a wave of discomfort. 'What?' she repeated.

Jules's eyes were sparkling. 'You're going to *the* Christmas charity ball. The one that the whole of New York talks about. It's on Saturday.' She looked back at Anissa and squeaked. 'It's on Saturday—and you don't have a dress!' A strange kind of smile came over her face and she put her hands on her hips. 'Well, aren't you just the original Cinderella.'

Anissa stood up from her bar stool. 'Okay, stop. You're making me nervous. Is this a big deal? I didn't know it was a big deal. Leo didn't make it sound like that. He just told me I needed a formal dress.'

Jules slapped her hand on her forehead. 'Mercy! The girl has a ticket to the hottest gig in town and doesn't even know it.' Her eyes ran up and down Anissa's length. 'Hmm...' It was almost as if something flashed through her brain. She clapped her hands together. 'You don't have a dress!'

Anissa frowned. 'You've said that—several times.'

Jules grabbed her jacket and bag, 'Come with me. Come with me now. I have the perfect thing. Perfect.'

Anissa couldn't think straight. Jules waved goodbye to her friends, jerked her hand and

Anissa had to stop to grab her own jacket before she was dragged out onto the cold street.

Jules kept muttering all the way along the street. 'This will be great. This will be perfect. It will suit you. Your name's written all over it.'

She pushed Anissa towards a building and led her up a flight of stairs to an apartment. As soon as Jules pushed open the front door Anissa sucked in a breath. It was like walking into another world.

There were mannequins everywhere, each wearing a unique dress design, each one a little more spectacular than the one next to it. And although Jules seemed to dress exclusively in black, there wasn't a single black item to be seen. Green. Blue. Red. Silver. Purple.

Anissa's foot hovered on the threshold. It was like the story from her childhood where the kids stepped through the back of a wardrobe into another world.

Jules seemed not to have noticed her hesitation. She marched straight over to a pale blue gown, glittering with jewels.

She turned to look at Anissa, her face filled with pent-up anxiety. 'What do you think?'

Anissa stepped inside, closed the door behind her and followed to where Jules was standing.

Jules paced around the mannequin.

'I made this for my fashion show. As soon as you said you needed a dress, it just flashed into my head. I can see you in it. I can see you in this dress. It's perfect. It suits your complexion and your eyes.' Jules pressed her hands together in front of her. 'What do you think? Would you consider it? Would you consider wearing one of my designs?'

Anissa couldn't talk. She couldn't think straight. She walked around the dress. It was pale blue with a sequined and beaded bodice with a slash neck, and a skirt made of layers and layers of pale blue tulle hanging completely straight. It was quite simply the most beautiful dress Anissa had ever seen.

She put her hand up to her chest. 'You want me to wear one of your designs?'

Jules immediately started babbling. 'Well, only if you want to. Only if you think it's good enough. But it would mean so much to me— having a dress I've designed worn by someone attending *the* Christmas ball of New York. It's my dream come true.'

Anissa couldn't believe her ears. The dress was stunning.

'You w-want me to wear…this?'

'Don't you like it?' Jules's voice was instantly defensive.

'I love it,' breathed Anissa. 'Will it fit?' she hardly dared to ask.

Jules nodded enthusiastically. 'Let's try it. As soon as I looked at you I thought it might work. We can make adjustments, if needed.'

Jules released the zipper at the back of the dress and slid it off the mannequin. She pushed Anissa towards her bedroom. 'Go in there. Try it on.'

Anissa stepped through to the bedroom. After a few hesitant moments she slipped off her clothes and tried the dress on. The satin lining slid over her skin easily. It felt almost like a second skin.

She couldn't fasten the zip so stepped back outside so Jules could do it for her.

Jules stood her in front of a full-length mirror and fastened the zip.

Anissa let out a little gasp. The dress was magnificent. The beaded and sequined bodice enhanced her neat curves, the slash neckline demure and flattering. The straight layers of tulle fluttered as she moved, swishing then falling back into place.

Jules put her hand up to her mouth. 'You look like an ice princess. It's just stunning.' She moved behind Anissa and nipped the dress in a little at the waist and grabbed a few pins. 'This needs only minor alterations.'

She finished pinning then stared into the mirror at Anissa's reflection, giving her a scrutinising glance. Next she shook out Anissa's blonde hair and pulled up the sides, leaving some tendrils around her ear. 'Have you thought about how you might get styled?'

Anissa was still staring at her reflection in an almost mesmerised way. 'Why would I need it styled?' she asked.

Jules pulled her hair a little tighter. 'What?'

Anissa let out a yelp as Jules bent around her. 'Tell me you are joking?'

Anissa tried to shake her head, but it was difficult when Jules had such a grip of her hair.

Jules let out a laugh. 'You really are a newcomer to all this, aren't you?' She sucked in a breath. 'Okay, do you trust me?'

Anissa looked at Jules and back to her reflection in the mirror. This dress was the most perfect thing she'd ever seen—and definitely the most gorgeous thing she'd ever worn. 'After you showing me this dress? Of course I trust you.' She turned from side to side as something flooded into her mind. 'He called me Ice Princess when we first met. And that's exactly how I feel in this dress. Like an ice princess.'

Jules was still eyeing her critically. 'Okay, it's just a few minor adjustments. I can do them in the next few days. Get yourself a pair of shoes.' She scribbled on a piece of paper. 'Heels no higher than this? Got it.'

Anissa nodded. This was all happening so fast.

Jules smiled. 'I have a friend who can do your hair and make-up. You'll be perfect.'

Anissa pressed her lips together. 'But after what happened today—what if this is all for nothing? What if he's changed his mind? What if doesn't want me to go any more?'

Jules shook her head. 'I've said it before and I'll say it again. This guy brought you to New York. He wants you to be his date for this ball. No matter what happened today, he'll still want you by his side.'

Anissa glanced back in the mirror. She liked how much she loved this dress, and how it made her look like someone else entirely. She gave a slow nod. 'Okay. I love this. Truly love it. How much do I owe you? This dress is spectacular. I can tell the hours and hours of work you've put into it.'

Jules shook her head. 'No. No way. All I want you to do is tell everyone who asks at the ball that the dress was designed by me. Give them my cards. I'll give you a whole pile.' She gave a broad smile. 'That's my dream come true.'

Anissa couldn't believe it. 'Really? You don't want me to pay you?'

Jules kept shaking her head. 'Honestly? You wearing my dress could give me so much publicity. It could really make me as a new designer.'

Anissa reached over and grabbed Jules's hands. 'Thank you so much for this. I don't know what I would have done without you.'

Jules put her hands on her hips and gave a slow nod of her head. 'It's my pleasure, but one thing. Have a think about Mr Billionaire. He might have whisked you off to New York, but don't let him take you for granted.' She raised her eyebrows. 'Maybe you should let him sweat a little about the dress. Let him think you haven't bought one.'

Anissa smiled. 'Jules, you have a wicked streak.'

Jules nodded. 'And I bet you do too…'

## CHAPTER SEVEN

LEO WAS FEELING like complete and utter crap. Just exactly as he should.

He'd left her. He'd left her alone in New York, a strange city where she knew practically no one. All because of one lousy freak-out in his head.

What was wrong with him? What if she couldn't get hold of her friend?

Up until that point they'd virtually had the perfect day. Anissa was interesting, fun and gorgeous. Everything he could ever ask for. And yet...

He'd let her down. He'd let them both down.

He stared at the phone for a few seconds. He'd almost picked it up at least dozen times now. He couldn't quite decide which one to phone—Noemi or Sebastian. Maybe he should phone both? Maybe he should phone neither?

But the constant texting between Anissa and her parents had set something off in his brain. She was part of a family. It didn't matter where she was in the world, or what she was doing, she was still part of a family and it was clear she loved it.

He had a different set of circumstances, but this constant feeling of not being good enough wasn't Noemi's or Sebastian's fault. It was down to his own upbringing, added to by his own misgivings. Every part of him was telling him to make an effort. And that wasn't just his business brain talking. Part of it was his heart.

Anissa was having an effect on him he hadn't expected.

He picked up the phone and dialled the numbers quickly. Noemi answered on the second ring. 'Leo? How are you? It's so nice to hear from you.'

She sounded genuinely happy to hear from him. Something spread through him. A warmth he hadn't really experienced before.

'Hi, Noemi,' he said as he settled back in the chair, 'I just wanted to check in...'

Anissa pulled out her phone as she headed from the subway. Although she wasn't used to New York, she felt safe. The streets were busy and well lit. Her phone buzzed again. It was Hans from the Championship Skiing Competition. They hadn't spoken properly in eighteen months. She couldn't imagine why he'd phone her twice in one day.

Last time she'd ignored the call. This time she pressed it to her ear.

'Hans?'

'Anissa! At last. Where are you?'

She looked around. It felt like a trick question. 'New York?'

'New York? What on earth are you doing in New York?'

She pulled a face, 'A holiday?' she answered, as if it was a question. What kind of answer did he expect?

'Darn it! I'm in Mont Coeur. I thought you were here.'

Her stomach crunched. Hans had gone to Mount Coeur to speak to her?

'Well, sorry. I've left for a few days.' She pressed her lips together for a second. 'Hans, did you want something?'

He cleared his throat. 'I was actually hoping to speak to you in person.'

Now she really was nervous. This seemed strange. 'What about?'

There was a long pause. 'It's just...that there's potentially an opening on the Skiing Championship Committee. I wanted to have a chat to see if you might be interested.'

She stopped walking. She was stunned.

'Wh-what?'

'I know we haven't spoken in a while,' Hans said smoothly, 'which is why I wanted to speak to you in person.'

She still couldn't really answer.

Hans kept talking. 'One of our members plans to resign in a few months—ongoing health issues—and we were talking about who would be perfect to take their place, and your name came up. We want someone young. We want someone who knows the sport inside out. They asked me to sound you out.'

Her head was spinning. Her name had come up? With the Skiing Championship Committee? She still couldn't quite believe it. She needed to clarify things.

'But what is it exactly that they wanted you to sound me out about?'

'It's probably better if we do this in person.'

Anissa looked around. She didn't know what to think. Her legs were actually shaking.

'When will you be back in Mont Coeur?'

'I don't know.' There was slight panic in her chest. 'I'll be in New York for at least the next four days.'

'Oh, okay.' Hans paused. 'How about if I email you some information and then we can chat when you're back in Mont Coeur. It will give you a few days to think about things and decide how you feel.'

Her brain was still in overdrive. She still wasn't exactly sure what he was saying to her. She stuttered out her email address.

Her heart gave a little leap as she hung up. She had no idea what this meant. But that horrible churning feeling in her stomach that had been there for the last year—the one that wondered if she would ever make it back to championship skiing again—suddenly lessened a bit. She'd never really considered other career opportunities. She actually didn't think there were any—apart from teaching skiing or being a chalet maid. This was different. Could this be the back-up plan that Leo had suggested to her?

This felt like the possibility of a light at the end of a very long tunnel.

Leo was pacing by the time he heard the elevator ping at the entrance to the penthouse. 'I'm sorry,' he said as soon as she stepped through the doors.

He'd spent the last few hours regretting his actions. He couldn't really explain them to himself so how on earth could he explain them to Anissa?

It all felt like too much. The stuff with his parents. The will. Meeting his brother and sister under difficult circumstances. And on top of all that—Anissa. He liked her. She was slowly but surely finding away under the shell he'd built around himself. He liked her laugh. He liked her questions. He liked her work ethic and her striving to do well.

But he also liked the way she clearly adored her parents and was in contact with them every day. He liked the way she always tucked a bit of hair behind her right ear. And he worried about how disappointed she would be if she didn't get back to championship skiing. He'd only known her a few weeks but he cared about her. He'd wanted her to enjoy herself in New York—and he'd almost ruined it today. All because of the torrent of emotion that had flooded over him.

He'd spent the last few hours feeling guilty, wondering where she was and hoping she would return. He'd had his phone in his hand so many times to try and call her—but that seemed ridiculous after he'd left her on her own.

It hadn't helped that an hour ago a delivery had arrived from the bakery store—twenty-four rich and gorgeous cupcakes. He hadn't ordered them, which meant that Anissa obviously had.

But now the constant ache in his stomach was gone. She was here.

Anissa's cheeks had a glow about them and

her eyes were sparkling. Her gaze narrowed and she got straight to the point. It seemed as if some time alone had focused her mind. 'Are you going to tell me what was wrong earlier?'

The words stuck somewhere in his throat. He'd been ready to churn out a whole load of excuses. But now that she was standing in front of him, her blonde hair peeking out from under hat, her blue coat fastened to her neck and dusted with snow, and her pale blue eyes focused entirely on him, his prepared excuses just seemed to disappear into the air around them. 'It's just…'

She unfastened her coat and hung it up. 'Just what?'

When he couldn't find the words, she gave a sigh. After a few seconds she walked into the kitchen, lifted the lid of the cupcakes box and gave a little nod. Then she grabbed a bottle of wine and took a glass from the cupboard. 'It's late, Leo. I'm tired. I… I had fun today. Or I thought we did. Until we didn't.'

She sighed as she poured the wine into a glass. 'Leo, you brought me here on the spur of the moment. You had business to do. You took me sightseeing. You brought me to stay in your penthouse. You invite me to a ball. Then you thrust your credit card at me and tell me to use it for the cab, drinks or…whatever I might like. You told me to use your credit card to shop. Have you any idea how insulting that is? As if…you're trying to buy me or something?'

Leo walked over to one of the windows. He stood with his hands in his pockets. In the darkness outside he could see all the glimmers of lights across the city. He wasn't used to sharing. He'd never really had anyone to confide in before. Today's conversation with Noemi had been…interesting. It finally felt as if he was starting to move in the right direction with his family. And now Anissa was asking him outright what was wrong.

Something caught his eye. A flicker to the side. A helicopter. New York was full of them.

It felt like an elephant had just put a foot on his chest.

Anissa appeared at his side, holding her glass of wine.

As he watched the light from the helicopter flicker across the sky the pain in his chest intensified. It was almost as if everything had finally come to a head and he just had to let it out.

'The family stuff.' His voice was croaky.

'Yes?' asked Anissa.

'I was in Mont Coeur for the reading of my mum and dad's will.' His words were stilted.

'Your parents died?' She was clearly surprised, 'I'm so sorry.'

He took a few moments to find the rest of his

words. 'I didn't even get a chance to know them.' His eyes fixed on the helicopter again. 'When they came to meet me in New York for the first time, they…they were killed in an accident.'

Anissa stepped in front of him, blocking out the blackness and twinkling lights of the city beyond. Concern was laced across her face. 'What kind of accident?'

The words choked in his throat. 'A helicopter crash. They died coming to meet me.'

He swayed just as Anissa's hands reached out to him. 'Leo.' Her wine sloshed on the floor as she guided him back to a chair.

He crumpled into the chair as the emotions that had been building inside him for the last few months bubbled over.

'If they hadn't discovered me, if they hadn't got in contact they would never have died. It was my fault. Mine. I should never have answered that letter. I should never have agreed to meet them.' Tears started to stream down his face.

Anissa knelt in front of him and took his hands in hers. 'Oh, Leo, I'm sorry. I'm so sorry. But it's not your fault. You could never have predicted something like that.' Her brow furrowed. 'But I don't understand. Why didn't you know your parents? You mentioned them before—but said they didn't bother much with you.'

He ran his fingers through his thick hair. 'I…

I… I didn't know them because they had me adopted as a baby. They weren't married, they had no support and they told me they'd had no choice but to give me up.'

She reached up and cradled his cheek with one hand. 'Oh, Leo,' she said softly.

It was the touch. The pure worry in her voice that gave him the strength to continue. 'I didn't know them. I didn't know them at all. My adoptive parents had always told me that I wasn't wanted—that I'd been abandoned. *They* were the ones who didn't bother much with me. I spent my whole life feeling not good enough— for them, or for my real parents.'

'But you were a kid. Why on earth would your adoptive parents tell you that? That's cruel.'

It was like a little light switching on in his head. He nodded. 'Yes, it is. It's how they were.' He straightened a little and put his hand over hers. 'They weren't really interested in me. I think the thought of having a kid was better than the actual experience. They always made me feel as if I was constantly a bother.'

'That's terrible. How dare they? Where are they now? Do you still talk?'

He shook his head. 'I left when I was twenty and never looked back. When I got the letter out of the blue from my real parents I was stunned. I didn't believe it at first. It took me a few weeks to get in touch.'

She nodded as if she could understand. 'And when you did?'

He took a deep breath and lifted his head. 'Salvo and Nicole were anxious to meet me. They said they'd been looking for me almost since they'd given me up. But they wanted a chance to tell Sebastian and Noemi about me. Apparently, they'd been so racked with guilt they hadn't told my brother and sister about me.'

She was almost afraid to ask. 'And did they get a chance?'

He gave a shudder. 'Not the way they wanted to. Noemi opened my reply. She confronted her mother about it. She was upset they'd kept me a secret—and, to be honest, so was I.'

'But you arranged to see them—to meet?'

A single tear snaked down his face. 'I did.' His voice broke again. 'I wanted to meet them, Anissa. I did. I'd never had a real family, not one where I felt as if I belonged, where I felt as if I was wanted. And then, all of a sudden, it seemed like it might happen.'

'Oh, Leo.' Her words were so soft, so full of empathy.

'And...then...' he shook his head '...they were gone. They'd arrived in New York a few hours early and decided to take a tour of the city in a helicopter.'

His hands were shaking. He couldn't help it.

'And then there was the funeral...'

Anissa's hand was warm on his cheek, the other clasping his hand. 'So you didn't meet Sebastian and Noemi then?'

He flung up his hands in exasperation. 'How could I? I wasn't sure what they knew about me. I didn't even know if Sebastian knew I existed. I could hardly reveal myself at the family funeral as the missing son.' He hated how this made his heart ache. 'I went. I just stayed at the back. There were hundreds of people there. I was just another Italian-looking guy in a suit. One of many.'

He hated how bitter and twisted that sounded, but he hated even more how bitter and twisted it made him feel.

'They must hate me. They must really hate me—Sebastian and Noemi. If my parents had never found me, they would never have been in New York. They would never have had the accident. Life would still be good. The business would still be in safe hands.' He sucked in a shaky breath. 'It's my fault. All my fault.'

This feeling had been sitting heavily over him like a dark cloak from the second the accident had happened. It haunted his dreams at night, had sat on his chest like a heavy weight during the funeral, and hindered every step he'd taken in the snow to go and meet his brother and sister.

Guilt was horrid. Guilt was like having something drain the life out of you slowly but surely. At least that's what it had been like the last few months.

'Of course it's not your fault, Leo. How could you have known? How could you ever have predicted that? It was just a horrible, horrible accident. And stop saying that. That's the second time you've said it. It's not your fault. Stop believing that.' She shook her head. 'You said they'd spent most of their lives searching for you. It sounds as if they would never have stopped.'

He tried to take in what she was saying. In his head he knew it probably made sense. But he just couldn't accept it. Not yet.

'From what you said about the funeral, it sounds like your parents were very popular.'

Leo nodded his head. 'Oh, they are—they were. You might have heard of them—the Cattaneos.'

A frown creased Anissa's brow and a second later he saw the flash of recognition in her eyes. Most people in Europe had heard of the Cattaneos.

'The jewellery people—your family are the jewellery people?'

He sighed and leaned back in the chair. 'Yeah. That's why things are so hard right now. They named me in their will.'

Anissa shook her head. 'But so they should, you are their son.'

Leo closed his eyes for a second. She made it sound so simple.

He let out a long, slow breath. 'Apparently, they did this a long time ago. They put a clause in their will to say that I have to assume the controlling stake in the family business for six months. If I don't accept it, or try and walk away during that time, the business gets dissolved.'

Anissa's eyes widened. 'What? No. That's terrible. It's an awful position for you to be in.'

He nodded. 'I know. Imagine how Sebastian and Noemi feel. Mystery brother appears out of nowhere and gets given the ability to ruin the family business completely. Is it any wonder Sebastian is angry? I can't help but imagine how I'd feel if the company I'd spend my life building got handed over to someone else.'

He leaned his head back against the leather recliner. 'I have no idea what happens next. I've been on my own for so long. But the question I have to ask myself is do I really want a family? My mother and father aren't there now, and they're the people I'd really wanted to form a relationship with. So, with Sebastian and Noemi, this hasn't been the best of starts. I've been left in a charge of their family business— how they can trust me, or me them? Let's face it, they have to be nice to me for the next six months—whether they want to or not.'

Anissa moved and sat on the edge of the chair next to him. After a few seconds she threaded her fingers through his hair. It was an intimate move. The move of someone who cared. 'Could it be that you're just feeling overwhelmed by everything? It sounds as though it's all happened so quickly. You didn't even get a chance to say goodbye to your parents properly.'

He was drawn by her touch. His hand automatically wound its way around her waist and he pulled her towards him, sliding her from the armrest and onto his lap.

She put her hands on either side of his head and pressed her forehead against his. 'Leo, who have you talked to about all this?'

He breathed slowly. 'Just my lawyers. I've been trying to find a way out without destroying the jewellery business.'

Her eyes fixed on his and she was so close her eyelashes were brushing against his skin. 'I meant who have you talked to about this for *you*, Leo. Not for business. Not for legal reasons. Who have you spoken to for you?'

He gave his head the slightest shake. 'No one.'

It sounded so lonely. It made it sound as if he had such a solitary existence.

Words choked in his throat. 'I've seen how close you are with your parents. I've never had anything like that. I don't even know how I should be with my brother and sister. I phoned Noemi earlier today. But it felt so stilted—not her, me. I just don't know how to have that kind of conversation. Not yet. Not while all this business stuff is hanging over our heads.'

'Leo, I can't imagine how hard this has been for you. And this time of year—Christmas—always seems to magnify things.' Her hands wove back through his hair and she gave him a smile. 'But I want to tell you one thing. You *are* good enough, Leo. You've always been good enough.'

Her lips brushed against his cheek and his head instinctively turned to capture her lips with his.

Heat flooded through him. There was so much electricity between them—it had been there from the very first time they'd met. But now it was more. It was deeper. The connection stronger. And he liked that. It meant so much. That feeling of finally connecting with someone. To want to feel her skin under his. He wanted to feel the heartbeat in her chest against his.

Whatever he'd done today, however mixed up and guilty he'd felt about everything, it seemed that Anissa had a more forgiving heart than he could have hoped for.

She tugged at his jumper, pulling it over his head as she stayed on his lap, matching his every kiss. Every cell in his body was roaring. It wasn't just the attraction. It was the empathy and understanding. Her words. Her reassurance. The complete and utter belief in her eyes when she'd looked at him and told him that he was good enough. It had made his heart soar in a way he'd never felt before.

This was new. This was all new to him.

And no matter what happened, whatever decision he made about the family business, something in his heart was telling him that for the first time in his life he'd found something that could be worth holding onto.

And as he picked Anissa up and carried her to his bedroom, he'd never felt surer of anything in his life.

# CHAPTER EIGHT

WOW. FOR THE first time in for ever her muscles ached in good ways instead of bad.

Last night she'd come home prepared to be angry at Leo. But one look at the expression on his face as he'd crumpled in front of her had almost been the end of her.

She'd had no idea what he'd been going through. She couldn't imagine the devastation of losing her parents—or the set of circumstances he'd described to her. Every part of the story had made her heart twist in her chest a little more at what Leo had missed out on. Every word had made her relish the good relationship she had with her parents. How must it feel to have never had that? And when it finally seemed like a possibility—to have it ripped away?

No wonder he was devastated. No wonder he was all over the place.

Now she understood the bravado and business face that Leo tried his best to keep in place. It was his mask. The thing that held him together.

Because he didn't have anyone else.

He didn't have anyone to share things with. His new-found relationship with his brother and sister had never had the chance to develop— and, thanks to the contents of the will, possibly never would.

But it was that overall feeling of not being good enough that she could relate to most.

It lit a little fire inside her. He was good enough. Surely his family would see that? Surely everyone could see it?

'Hey.'

The voice beside her made her start. She rolled over in the bed to face a sleepy-eyed Leo. Darn, he was sexy in the morning.

'Hey,' she replied as her lips automatically turned upwards.

'What do you want to do today?' he said huskily.

'Do I still get to play tourist?' She was almost holding her breath, wondering what he would say.

'Absolutely. Tell me where you want to go today and I'll take you. Tonight I'd really like it if you'd come with me when I have dinner with a business associate.'

'You would? Do you think he'll be okay with me being there?'

'He'll have to be. Joe is the reason I came back. He's playing hard ball on a business proposal that I thought we'd wrapped up.' Leo lifted one of her hands and kissed it. 'Who wouldn't want a smart, intelligent lady at their table? He'll have to understand that I'm entertaining my guest. Anyway, I think he'll like you. Who wouldn't?'

She couldn't help but be flattered. Chalet girl by day…girlfriend by night? She still wasn't quite sure.

She nodded. 'Where's dinner? What do I need to wear?'

He pulled a face and groaned. 'Did I make a huge mess of things yesterday, giving you a credit card and telling you to buy something?'

She nodded. 'You might have done. But don't worry. The ballgown is sorted.' She'd been offended before when he'd said his PA would find her something, but now she'd much rather sightsee than spend the day shopping. It was time for a compromise. 'How about you give me the number of your PA and I can tell her what size I am, what colour I prefer and what style of dress I like. I'm pretty easygoing and, as long as it fits and covers me, I'll wear it. That way neither of us has to go near a clothes store today.' She leaned a little closer. 'Anyway, I'm all about the water today. I have something much more fun in mind.'

One of his eyebrows rose. 'The water?' He was obviously curious.

She nodded but didn't give anything away.

Leo leaned over to kiss her. 'Your wish is my command. Now, let's go and have some fun.'

It only took her ten minutes to get ready and have the conversation with Leo's PA. She switched on the coffee machine while Leo was showering and fired up his computer to check her messages.

Her heart gave a little leap as she noticed the email from Hans straight away.

The email was detailed. It gave her a full outline of what her role and responsibilities would be. They had a clear job description for her with a wide remit, complete with salary and expenses—more than she could ever have imagined. She'd be right at the heart of the championship skiing committee.

But not as a competitor.

Part of it made her feel happy. She'd never have thought they would have considered her in a million years. But the other part of her brain was irrationally insulted. They assumed she'd never get back to professional skiing. Surely they knew she was training again?

Almost automatically her hand started rubbing her leg and her other hand reached for her handbag and froze. She was looking for painkillers. The ones she took every day.

The ones she currently didn't need.

She stopped and pushed herself up from the chair, filling a glass with water while she waited for the coffee. Taking the painkillers had become automatic.

Except for...now.

She did a few gentle stretches. The truth was since she'd got on her feet again she'd never stopped training. She'd thought she just had to learn to live with pain and medicate it.

She'd never actually imagined that if she'd stopped skiing the pain wouldn't be there any more. How stupid was that?

The machine clicked next to her and she exchanged Leo's full cup of coffee with her empty one. She inserted a new pod and pressed the button as she tried to process her thoughts. Was she reaching for something she could never achieve? Was she damaging her body for a dream that would never come true?

Tears pricked in her eyes as she looked out over the snow-dusted city. Out there was a world of possibilities. Maybe she needed to

consider her options a little more rationally—
take the emotion, history and heart out of
things—but could she do that?

Leo appeared at the door smiling, rubbing his
hair with one towel, another wrapped around
his waist.

He fixed on her with those bright blue eyes.
'Brilliant, I smell coffee.' His fresh, clean scent
drifted around her as he moved beside her and
shot her a sexy grin. 'So, Anissa. Surprise me.
What are we doing today?'

She was definitely infectious. And he liked it.
He liked it a lot.

They started by taking the Staten Island
Ferry past the Statue of Liberty. But one sight-
ing wasn't enough and Anissa wanted to do
the whole tourist thing. So they took the boat
to Liberty Island and climbed the stairs to the
pedestal, statue and finally the crown.

'Isn't it great?' she whispered as they looked
out over New York Harbor and Manhattan.

'It is, isn't it?' he agreed, wondering why he'd
never done this before.

She nudged him. 'It's freezing today. Do you
think the Hudson will be frozen?'

He thought for a second. 'Parts of it could
be—why?'

She smiled. 'Because it might make where I want to go next even more special.'

'And where's that?'

She kept grinning. 'Not saying. I want it to be a surprise,' she said teasingly. 'I've checked the directions and I'll tell you when we get there.'

An hour and a half later he frowned as he looked at a sign in front of him. 'You want to go here? Really?'

'Are you joking?' She held up her hands. 'Of course I want to go here.' She pointed to the river. 'Look, a submarine surrounded by frozen ice, how cool is that?' She gestured to the hangar high above them. 'In there is a space shuttle. Have you ever seen a space shuttle before? Touched one? I haven't. And I can't wait.' She spun around and pointed directly above. 'And up there, are the old war planes. Don't you remember that movie? The one where the guy is the last man left in New York with the zombies and he plays golf from the top of one of the war planes?'

Leo frowned, taking a few seconds to place the film, before it finally clicked in his brain. 'Of course!' He grabbed her hand and pulled her towards him. 'You're just a big kid really, aren't you?'

Her cold nose brushed against his chin.

'Maybe I am,' she said quickly. 'Or maybe I'm just reassessing things. Deciding what's important.'

The look in her eyes as she said the words tugged at his heart. There it was again. The sign that they were on the same wavelength. She lifted her hands and rested them on his shoulders. She licked her lips. 'Maybe we both need to have a think about things. Tell me more about your chat with Noemi yesterday.'

He rolled his eyes. He couldn't help it. 'It was fine. She was chatty. Asked lots of questions. Mainly around when I'd be back.'

Anissa nodded her head. 'She wants to get to know you better, Leo. It's a natural response. And I'm glad.'

He nodded. 'I guess. It was apparently a dream of Mother and Father's that they would have all their children together around the table at Christmas.'

Anissa took a few seconds. 'Does Noemi want to fulfil that dream?'

He nodded. 'But isn't it too late? They're gone.'

She gripped his shoulders firmly. 'But you're not gone. Noemi and Sebastian are not gone. This is your family, Leo. The people you should get to know. The people you should get to love.'

She was right. He knew she was right. But it just seemed like such a big leap into the unknown.

She kept talking. 'Christmas is a really special for families. I always love spending this time of year with my mum and dad.'

'Are you going home for Christmas?' Something panged inside him. He wasn't quite sure how he wanted her to answer this question.

She shook her head. 'I promised I'd work. I'm going home a few days before Christmas then coming back on the twenty-third. It will be fine. My mum will make Christmas dinner early and we'll celebrate then.' She gave a shrug. 'I always keep my commitments and someone has to work.'

She'd be there. Inside his heart gave a little leap. If he decided to go back for Christmas, Anissa would be there. Somehow that made things not seem quite so daunting.

She tilted her head to one side. 'Noemi was the easy one to call, wasn't she? The person you really need to call is Sebastian.'

He let out a wry laugh. 'How come you never beat around the bush? How come you just go straight for the jugular?'

She laughed too. 'Because life is too short. And, anyway, you know your brother was angry about the will. I bet he was hurt. He must have spent his whole life working for that position and now he feels as if it's been ripped away from him and all his hard work counts for nothing.' She wrinkled her nose. 'What's Noemi's stake in this?'

'She's a silent partner. But I'm not sure how happy she is about that.'

Anissa put her hand on his chest. 'You don't know what else is going on in their lives—apart from the fact they've just lost their parents and found out about a secret brother, there could be other stuff.' She stood up on her tiptoes and whispered in his ear as she hugged him tight. 'Take a breath, Leo. Take a chance. Once they get to know you, they'll think that you're great.'

His stomach gave a flutter. He'd never, ever had anyone support him as much as Anissa was doing now. And he wanted to reciprocate. He wanted to do the same for her as she was doing for him.

But that could mean asking her questions she didn't want to be asked. Asking if her she really could make it back to championship skiing. And right now the last thing he wanted to do was hurt her. Or damage the most valuable relationship he'd started to form.

He kissed her swiftly on the lips and lowered his voice. 'Okay, tourist, how would you like to see the inside of my submarine?'

She laughed. 'Now, how could any girl resist an offer like that?'

* * *

Five hours later they'd just had enough time to dash back to the apartment and dress for dinner. Anissa hadn't checked to see what Leo's PA Keisa had sent over. She'd just grabbed the hangar and rushed into her room to shower and change. She blasted her hair with the dryer and applied some make-up quickly. Her heart gave a little flip at the box of shoes on the bed. Black patent leather stilettos with red soles. Probably cost more than she earned in a month. She unzipped the clothes bag and shook out the dress.

It was gorgeous—red, a colour she rarely wore. It had a straight neckline, falling from her hips with a small red flounce around the bottom stopping at her knees.

She stepped into the dress and the shoes and took one quick glance in the mirror before hurrying out to Leo.

'Wow.' He was standing waiting for her in a dark suit and tie, a glass of red wine in his hand. The lights in the penthouse were dimmed and she loved the way his eyes sparkled as she sashayed towards him.

She gestured down, 'Well, I haven't met Keisa but she sure has impeccable taste.'

Leo nodded appreciatively. 'She does.' Then he gave a little smile. 'I might have sent her a photo.'

'Of me?' She was surprised. 'When?'

'Today.' He shrugged. 'We took masses of pictures at the statue and the Natural History Museum the other day.'

She moved forward and tapped his chest. 'And I have a spectacular photo of you pretending to hold a giant blue whale from the other day.'

He laughed. 'I forgot about that one. You could use it as blackmail material.' Then he nodded and wagged his finger. 'Actually, I have a really good picture of someone with their head inside a T-Rex's mouth. Now, *that* would be a good blackmail picture.'

She slid her arms up around his neck. 'You'd really blackmail me?'

His hands rested on her hips and his gaze was loaded. 'I could be persuaded not to.'

She moved closer, so she could feel the full length of his body against hers. 'Tell me about tonight. Tell me about Joe.'

He met her gaze. 'Are you worried about dinner?'

She pulled a face. 'Not worried, really. But… I know this is a big deal for you. I don't want to say anything wrong. Is there anything I should avoid?'

He shook his head. 'Just be yourself. You're perfect. Joe will love you.'

It was like warm honey spreading through

her. Since he'd opened up to her last night it was as if all the walls had come down. He seemed easier, more relaxed. She didn't doubt he was still considering what to do next about his family, but the dark, hooded look had left his face. It was almost as if he was relieved to have finally shared how he was feeling about things.

She stepped back and slipped her hand into his. 'Come on, then, Mr Baxter, take me to dinner.'

It was his favourite restaurant—and it was Joe's too. The restaurant slowly rotated as they ate, meaning that in the space of an hour they got to see all the views of New York.

Service was smooth and quick. And just like he'd predicted, Joe was charmed by Anissa. It was the first time Leo had ever taken a date with him to a business meeting but somehow this had just felt right.

Anissa had enchanted Joe with stories about her childhood in Austria, and then intrigued him with tales about her international skiing experiences.

As she spoke Leo couldn't help but notice the far-off look in her eye or the slightly wistful tone in her voice. He wasn't quite sure what to say or how to react. As their main courses arrived, she turned towards both of them.

'I've had an interesting job offer.'

'You have?'

She nodded hesitantly. 'From someone I used to have a lot of dealings with—there's a vacancy on the International Skiing Championship Committee.' She seemed a little nervous. 'They've considered me.'

Joe leaned over and squeezed Anissa's hand. 'Of course they have. They know talent when they see it.' He seemed to pick up the fact she didn't reply right away. 'They've considered you—are you considering them?'

It was the careful way Joe turned the question around. He was a wily character with years of experience in dealing with people. Leo held his breath. He wanted to know the answer to that question too. Anissa hadn't mentioned the job offer earlier—why not?

She toyed with the food on her plate. 'I'm not sure,' she said finally.

Leo couldn't help himself. 'Why not? It sounds wonderful.'

She gave a little sigh. 'Because if I say yes, that's it. It's almost like I'm saying I'll never compete any more—I'll never get the gold medal. I don't quite know if I'm ready to do that.'

Joe nodded. 'You said earlier you had an accident. Do you honestly think you'll get back to championship level?'

Leo shifted in his seat. He'd asked Anissa to consider a back-up plan, but he hadn't been quite as blunt. It seemed that Joe's age allowed him to be me much more direct.

Anissa's face was blank. She didn't reply.

Joe gave her hand a squeeze again and waved his other hand. 'Well, whatever you decide I'm sure it will be right for you. After all, you need to do what makes you happy.' He picked up his wine glass and raised it in a toast towards Anissa. 'To Anissa, a beautiful woman with a beautiful future, whatever it may be.'

Anissa picked up her glass and raised it back to Joe, tentatively taking a sip. She looked sad. She looked unsure. And Leo hated that for her.

His heart gave a squeeze as his head finally caught up.

He loved her. For the first time in his life he actually loved someone.

He wanted her to be happy. He wanted her to know she was good enough, and to choose the career path that was right for her. But more than anything he wanted her to be with him.

It was almost like someone had just lit up the sky behind him with fireworks.

He lifted his glass and clinked it against hers. 'To Anissa,' he agreed. 'You can be whatever you want to be.'

She met his gaze. Her eyes still looked unsure. But he'd never more sure of anything in his life.

Joe was an old charmer. He could be brash, he could be flattering, and he could definitely charm the birds from the trees. Business between him and Leo had been wrapped up within five minutes. There had been a few disagreements backwards and forwards but no bad blood. It was clear that both men respected each other and she liked that. She liked it that Joe respected Leo's business acumen. Joe thought Leo was good enough. And that made her happy.

Dinner finished relatively early and since it wasn't far to Leo's apartment they waved the car away.

She extended one leg and pointed to her shiny new shoes. 'You do know that walking on these red soles essentially ruins them.'

Leo frowned. He obviously didn't get it. 'But shoes are for walking in. What else are you supposed to do with them?'

She shook her head. 'Never mind. Let's walk.'

His hand slid around her waist, pulling her closer.

She decided to ask the question she'd wanted to ask all night. 'Have you had any more thoughts about what to do about your family?'

He pressed his lips together for a second. 'Well, you're right. I probably should talk to Sebastian at some point—try and reassure him that I'm not interested in taking his place at the company.' He sighed. 'I've already told him, but I don't know if he's ready to listen yet.'

'Are you sure you don't want to be part of the family business?'

'What do you mean?'

She stopped walking for a second and looked at him. The Italian blood in him was strong, his sallow skin, his dark ruffled hair. His bright blue eyes were startling. His lithe body and build. He was Italian through and through. Even if he hadn't found out his ancestry, she could have guessed it.

'This is your family business too, Leo. Your mother and father left you the controlling shares for a reason. They loved you. You were their son. They wanted you to be part of the business—to work with them and your brother and sister. Do you really want to walk away from this, without thinking about it properly?'

He had a confused look in his eyes and he shook his head slowly. 'How can I? How can I take away what is theirs?'

She gripped his arm. 'Because it's yours too.' She stopped for a second and took a deep breath. 'Don't just walk away without thinking about it. Sebastian's reaction is making you feel as if you're not entitled to this. But you are, Leo. I don't want you to walk away and then regret it years down the line.'

She couldn't help the passion in her voice. Last night they'd connected. She'd seen how broken he'd been—how confused. But what she could also see was the yearning to belong. To be part of a family.

Her heart ached for this gorgeous man who tried to hide his emotions. Maybe waiting the six months then walking away from the family business was exactly what he should do. But she didn't know that. And, more importantly, Leo didn't know that.

She didn't pretend to have a head for business. But Leo clearly did. He might have ideas and skills that could enhance the business. If only he would take the time to speak to Sebastian. If they could put the family business aside and get the chance to get to know one another.

She sucked in a slow breath. She was an only child and, like most only children, had longed for a brother or sister. How would she feel if she found out now that she did have one?

She knew in her heart she'd want to know everything about them. But Leo still hadn't answered her question. His brow was furrowed as if he was mulling over what she'd said. Something clicked in her brain.

'Your brother, Sebastian. You said you didn't meet his family because they hadn't arrived yet.'

He nodded. 'Yes.'

'Do you have a niece or a nephew?'

'I have…a nephew, I guess.' He honestly looked as though he really hadn't processed that. 'I'd never really considered the fact I was an uncle.'

'What's his name? What age is he?'

'His name is Frankie. He's…two, I think.'

Anissa clapped her hands together. 'A two-year-old nephew? That's brilliant.' She tugged at Leo's arm. 'You do know that New York has some of the best toy stores in the world.'

Now he looked really confused. 'Wh-what?'

She put a hand on each of his arms. 'Leo, in a few weeks' time it's Christmas. Whether you decide to go back to Mont Coeur or not, what you can't do…' she shook her head fiercely '…what you absolutely can't do is ignore the fact that this is the first Christmas you've known about your nephew. You have to get him something—just like you got something for Keisa.'

She gave him a little shake. 'This time, Leo, it's not a present for your loyal PA. This time it's for family. A nephew is a gift.'

It was as if a light came on in his eyes. His lips turned up slightly. 'So,' he said slowly. 'I have to go gift shopping?'

She nodded. 'Finally, you're getting it.'

He held out his hands. 'What on earth do I buy a two-year-old boy?'

She winked at him. 'You should know. You used to be one.'

He groaned but she wouldn't let him away with it. She pointed one finger and pressed it into his chest with every word. 'You. Are. Going. To. Be. A. Great. Uncle.'

He put his hand to his chest. 'I am going to be a bruised uncle.'

She glanced at her watch. 'Darn it, the toy stores will be closed by now.'

Leo raised his eyebrows and pulled out his phone. 'Most places can be persuaded to open. Particularly if you'll make a charitable donation to a place of their choosing.'

Her heart gave a little leap and after a five-minute conversation Leo hailed a cab and named one of the most well-known toy stores. 'We're in luck,' he said as they climbed in. 'Apparently, it's a major stocktake night on the run-up to Christmas. Staff are already there.' There was a gleam in his eyes. 'We can go in.'

'Brilliant.' She rubbed her hands together as

the cab wound its way through the snowy New York streets.

The lights were still on in the toy store but the shutters were pulled across the storefront. A member of staff was watching and waved them round to side entrance. He held out his hand. 'Leo Baxter?'

Leo nodded and shook his hand. 'Thanks for doing this.'

The man laughed. 'Anyone who'll make that big a donation to the children's cancer foundation gets my attention. Do you want one of the staff to help you shop—or do you just want to look around on your own?'

Leo glanced back at Anissa. She was already dying to find her way around the toy store. 'I think we're good.' She nodded.

The manager smiled and waved his arm. 'In that case, enjoy yourselves.'

She couldn't help herself and clapped her hands together excitedly. 'Come on, Leo. Let's go.'

Leo seemed a bit bewildered by the packed aisles and colourful signs everywhere. They moved from computers, to board games, to action figures, cars, laser guns and then on to game consoles, bikes, skateboards, roller skates and outdoor play furniture. Leo shook his head. 'I've just no idea where to start. I've never even met the kid.'

He sighed. 'And if he's anything like his dad, he'll probably hate me.' She hated the defeated look in his eyes. She walked over and wrapped one hand around his neck and ran the other through his hair. 'Leo Baxter, stop thinking like that. Stop thinking the glass is half-full. Start thinking about the whole new adventures you could be having.'

Being around him tonight had given her a spurt of new energy. She wanted to help Leo believe in who he was. She wanted him to know his value as part of the family.

He put his hands around her waist and spoke quietly. 'The truth is I could buy the entire contents of this store. But what good would that do?'

She nodded. 'You're right. What you need to do is think of something you loved as a kid. Something you would want to buy for your own son.' She gave a playful shrug. 'If you ever have one.'

His eyes locked onto hers, his gaze intense. For a second it took her breath away. It was almost like he was staring right into her very soul. Seeing every part of her. No one had looked at her like that—ever.

His voice was husky. 'How come you didn't tell me about the job offer?'

The words took her by surprise.

Of course. She hadn't told him. Because she hadn't really had time to think about it properly yet. It had just come out in the course of the conversation with Joe this evening.

When she didn't answer straight away, Leo started talking again. 'It sounds like a great opportunity. They must think a lot of you if they got in touch. Wouldn't you love to do something like that?'

She could see genuine enthusiasm in his eyes and her stomach coiled as she knew it wasn't mirrored in her own. 'I… I…don't know,' she stumbled.

Leo was still enthused. 'They obviously think you have the knowledge, the skill set and the respect of the skiing community to offer you a position like that. Just think how much you could influence things, shape the future of professional skiing.'

*But I won't have a gold medal.*

The thought seemed to be implanted in her brain. It had felt as if it had been on a loop from the moment that Hans had called her.

Maybe she was being ridiculous, but she just couldn't shake that thought.

Leo was still talking all about how wonderful she would be. What a brilliant opportunity it was. Encouraging her to be the best she could be.

All of a sudden she felt overwhelmed. New

York had been fabulous. But her whole life was upside down. She couldn't concentrate long enough to make any decisions. And in amongst all this she'd met a wonderful man who'd shared some really personal moments with her and maybe even stolen a little part of her heart.

Had she really just thought that? After only a few weeks?

She gulped. Leo was still talking. She gave herself a little shake and patted her hand against his chest. 'Hey. We can't stay here all night. The staff will need to get home. What was your number one toy as a kid?'

Right now she would do anything to distract him from the subject of her, and her job offer.

For the briefest second he looked a little surprised at her interruption, but then there was a flash in his eyes. 'Dinosaurs!' he exclaimed. 'Dinosaurs were the thing I absolutely loved.'

'Of course,' she agreed quickly. 'What kid doesn't love dinosaurs?' She grabbed his hand. 'Come on, I'm sure they're just around the corner.'

Ten minutes later they had a mat with volcanoes, jungles and rivers, along with every dinosaur that the store stocked. Leo's arms were full.

Anissa bent down and picked up a few human

figures and a toy jeep. She laughed. 'Collateral damage. We need some people that the dinosaurs can eat.'

'Good idea,' he agreed as they headed to the cash desk. His footsteps faltered and he turned to face her. 'Anissa?'

'Yes?'

He took a moment. 'Thank you.'

'What for?'

'For this. For thinking about Frankie. For being there for me. For everything.' His voice cracked a little.

It was like a vice gripping her heart. She didn't want him to say anything else. Wasn't ready for anything else. She was still getting used to the fact her leg and back didn't ache constantly. She was still trying not to think about what her life could look like. Most of all, she was still trying to work out how she felt about the gorgeous billionaire who'd whisked her halfway around the world.

She painted a smile on her face. 'That's what friends are for.'

# CHAPTER NINE

THE LAST FEW days had been good, but even though physically they were closer than ever, emotionally Anissa felt distant. At times Leo watched her staring off into space, clearly mulling things over—things that she wasn't sharing with him.

It felt as if it was time to take some action. To try and let her see herself as he saw her. Not as a sportswoman who'd had an accident and had had her dreams snatched from her fingers but as a beautiful, intelligent woman who could re-evaluate her life and what she wanted to achieve.

When he'd seen the hurt in her eyes as she'd talked about her accident, he'd imagined that taking her away from Mont Coeur would give her a chance to rethink things. A chance to see what her life could be like outside skiing. But it seemed that Anissa was still fixated on that gold medal. He hated the fact that he wondered if it would actually be in her reach or not.

'Anissa?' he asked. 'How are you doing?'

She'd disappeared for a few hours to get her hair and make-up done for the Christmas charity ball, then as soon as she'd returned she'd ducked into one of the other rooms to change. He still wasn't sure what she would be wearing. All he knew was that his credit card only had a charge for a pair of shoes, and that made him *really* nervous.

'I'm fine,' came the muffled voice from inside the room.

'Need any help?'

There was a long minute's silence and then the door opened. 'Nope,' she said simply as she stepped towards him.

His breath caught somewhere in his throat. Anissa's blonde hair was piled on top of her head with a few loose tendrils around her face. She was wearing a pale blue floor-length dress, with beads and sequins on the bodice and skirts that seemed to shimmer as she walked.

It was like she'd cast a magic spell all around him. 'You look like an ice princess,' he breathed.

She smiled as she stepped up to him. 'That's what you called me in Mont Coeur. I kept it in mind.'

There was a tiny shimmer of glitter on her cheeks. Her lips were a rich rose colour, and her eyelashes longer than he'd ever seen them.

'Where on earth did you get this dress? It's perfect, the exact colour of your eyes.'

She looked down and held out the skirts. 'I can't quite believe it. Do you remember me telling you about Chloe's cousin being in New York? Turns out she's a fashion student. When she found out where I was going, she asked if I'd consider one of her dresses.' She spun around, letting the light catch the few scattered sequins on the skirts.

Leo's heart tightened in his chest. She looked stunning. She was stunning. Inside and out. And tonight, at some point, he was going to tell her how he felt about her.

He gave her a bow. 'Okay, Ms Lang. Let me take you to New York's finest ball.'

It was everything she could ever have dreamed of. The black limousine pulled up to a red carpet outside the famous hotel. Cameras flashed instantly. It seemed the ball was even more prestigious than she'd thought. As soon as they entered the foyer Leo started nodding to people. It only took a few seconds for a woman to grab hold of her arm. 'Your dress. It's exquisite. Who is the designer?'

Anissa smiled. 'Oh, it's someone new. Her name is Jules Chen.' She looked down at the pale blue gown. 'I think she'll be the next big thing.'

The woman nodded in agreement. 'Well, if your dress is anything to go by, I'd say she will be.'

Anissa felt a little swell of pride as she pressed Jules's card into the woman's hand. She'd need to tell Jules.

Leo led her further through the foyer. The ballroom had a beautiful curved staircase on either side, leading down to the black-and-white floor.

As if they'd planned it especially for her, the lighting was blue and gold, and the huge chandeliers above sent a myriad of rainbow lights across all the walls. The whole room was decorated for Christmas, with strings of elegant twinkling lights. Slim and unusual white Christmas trees were decorated with glittering blue baubles, and blue and gold garlands were wound around the pillars in the middle of the room.

From the second they arrived waiters with silver trays appeared with glasses of champagne and trays of tiny food she couldn't even identify.

A large orchestra had been set up in one

of the adjoining rooms and the music flowed through the ballroom.

Leo introduced her to couple after couple, each one more glamorous than the one before. Dozens of people asked about her dress and each time she told them Jules's name and pressed a card into their hand she felt a little buzz of excitement. Hopefully the more people who heard her name, the more people would talk about her and seek out her designs. Finally, after they'd talked to everyone and circled the edges of the ballroom more than once, he turned to her and extended his hand. 'May I have this dance?'

She smiled and placed her glass of champagne on one of the tables. 'I thought you'd never ask.'

As the music started around them he led her into the middle of the dance floor. Dancing was formal, with most couples in traditional waltz holds. 'You know how to do this?' she asked as her stomach gave a few flips.

'Don't you?' He grinned down at her.

'Let's just say I didn't have much time in the past for balls,' she said wryly.

He bent to her ear, his lips brushing against her. 'It's easy,' he whispered. 'Just follow my lead.'

And so she did. He steered her elegantly

around the dance floor to the popular slow Christmas pop song. It seemed that even famous balls couldn't escape the clichéd cheesy pop ballads. But she liked this one, and naturally picked up the rhythm and tempo of the steps.

'Told you I could teach you,' he joked.

'If you can ski, you can do anything,' she answered with false bravado.

His eyebrows rose. 'Is that so?' Before she could think any further he spun her around, turn after turn, until the whole ballroom was flashing before her eyes. She leaned her head forward onto his chest. 'Stop,' she groaned. 'I feel dizzy.'

'I haven't even started yet,' he joked as he slowed their steps. 'Hey,' he continued. 'You can always just stand on my shoes.'

'With these heels? I'd spear you to the floor.'

He spun her once again, still laughing, her skirts swirling out around them and the sequins on her dress glimmering in the pale blue lights. She felt like a princess. And definitely not an ice princess. Her heart was beating so fast she thought it could power the whole of Manhattan.

No one had made her feel like this before. Alain had never made her heart beat like this— and he'd never her treated like this. It didn't take money to treat a girl like a princess—or to make her feel that way.

Leo, no matter what else he was going through, seemed to do this seamlessly.

Every look, every smile made each cell in her body stand to attention. She couldn't deny the attraction between them—or the buzz of electricity that seemed to sizzle around them.

But what were Leo's expectations of her?

She could see people looking at them as they danced past. With his tall and broad frame, Italian looks and bright blue eyes he was easily the best-looking man in the room. The guy was a billionaire. And he was with her.

Anissa Lang. Chalet girl and ski instructor. Why? Why had he chosen her?

If she hadn't slipped that night when practising it was likely that they would never have met. Never have made that connection. If she hadn't been assigned to clean his chalet they might never have seen each other again.

That made her stomach squirm. A series of coincidences had brought them together. What did that really mean?

She could sense herself rapidly losing her heart to this guy. A guy who stayed in New York. A guy who had success at his fingertips.

Why would he consider a girl who didn't even know what she wanted out of life?

The thoughts started to overwhelm her. Maybe she was reading too much into all this.

Maybe once Leo had time to think and resolve the issues he had with his family he would forget all about her.

Her chest tightened. That scared her. The thought of never seeing Leo again? The thought of never being around him made her stomach twist in a way she hadn't expected.

He was still smiling at her with those bright blue eyes. He held out his arm and spun her underneath it, sliding his arm around her waist and leading her off the dance floor.

'Let's take a break,' he said smoothly. 'We need to talk.'

It was weird. She thought she could hear the beating of her heart in her ears. How was that even possible?

They moved out of the now-crowded ballroom, past the orchestra, and through to another room that looked out over part of Central Park.

He took her hand in his. 'I called Sebastian today.'

'You did?'

He nodded. 'When you went to get your hair and make-up done, I decided it was time.'

Her heart swelled a little. She knew how wary he'd been about making that call. 'How was it?'

He pressed his lips together. 'Still a bit awkward. I'm just not sure where, or if, I fit in this family.'

She nodded slowly. 'But you're taking steps. That's the point.'

He sucked in a deep breath. 'That's what I want to talk about.'

Her skin prickled as if a cool breeze had swept over her skin. She wasn't quite sure where this was heading. 'What do you mean?'

'Steps. I'm not sure what comes next with… my family.' He stumbled over the last words. 'But all that stuff—finding my real parents, then losing them—has given me a chance to re-evaluate my life. To look at what I want. To decide what I want to do with it.'

His words were coming out quicker. He was getting more excited.

Anissa's mouth was dry. 'What do you want to do with it?'

He took her other hand. 'It's more about who I want to do it with.'

She could almost swear her heart stopped beating.

Her voice was barely audible. 'Wh-what?'

Leo's eyes were sparkling and his smile wide. He closed both hands over hers. 'I want to do it with you, Anissa. Stay with me. Stay with me in New York. Have a clean break from your past life and take your time to decide what you want to do. You've been different these last few days. It's like the shadows have lifted from your eyes and you've come out from under a cloud.'

Her heart twisted at those words—partly because they might be true—but Leo kept talking, his enthusiasm brimming over.

'Stay with me. Take some time. Decide what you want to do and where you want to be. We both know that you might not make it back to gold-medal level again. But you're brilliant, Anissa. There's a world of opportunities out there for you. You just need to decide which one you want. So take your time. Stay with me. Get away from the slopes. New York could give you the time and space you need to make some plans for the future.'

She bristled at those words. He'd said her fear out loud. He'd said that she likely wouldn't get back to the standard she needed to get the gold medal. It had played on her mind constantly for the last year—everyone had spoken with their silent disappearance from her life—but Leo was the first person to actually say the words to her face. And she didn't like them.

Leo reached up and touched her cheek. 'Please tell me you'll stay, Anissa. Now I've found you, I don't want to lose you. I love you.'

Her heart burned in her chest. Part of her

wanted to shout out in joy and part of her wanted to burst into tears.

She'd met someone she'd connected with. Someone who, with one glance, could set her pulse racing. She'd seen into his pain, into his feelings of inadequacy, and completely understood. What's more, she'd wanted to help. She hated that this wonderful, caring man felt like that.

Maybe she should be laughing. Maybe she should be throwing her arms around his neck and telling him that she loved him too.

Because she did.

But she just couldn't. Not now. Not here. Not when he'd just said those other words.

It didn't matter that it was the most romantic setting. It didn't matter that most of other women in room would think she was crazy.

She wasn't ready to give up on her dreams. It just seemed too much. Those slow feelings of being overwhelmed that had developed in the last few days were now gathering speed like snow tumbling down a mountain in an avalanche.

She could almost hear a ringing in her ears. The tightness across her chest had spread. Although she could breathe in, she was struggling to get it back out. Her head started to swim.

She stepped back. Out of his reach, out of the

smell of his deep woody aftershave and away from the heat emanating from his body.

She needed space. She needed time.

His eyes widened as if he'd finally realised something was wrong.

'Anissa?'

She pulled her hands back against her chest and shook her head.

There was noise behind them. An ornamental clock striking midnight.

It was like the spur she needed.

She shook her head and gathered her skirts in her hands. 'No, Leo.' The words choked halfway in her throat. 'I'm sorry.'

As she headed to the stairs she stumbled and tripped, leaving one of her silver jewelled sandals behind. For a second she hesitated, wondering if she should pick it up. But Leo was still staring at her, his face a picture of confusion.

She couldn't take the chance he would come after her—would try to persuade her to stay.

Tears clouded her vision. She had to get away before the pressure in her chest became too much. She turned and fled down the stairs as the last strike of midnight sounded.

Leo was stunned. What had just happened?

One second he was inviting the woman that

he loved to stay with him. The next second she was crying and running away.

For a few seconds he was frozen to the spot, wondering how he could have got things so wrong. Wondering if he'd completely misread where he and Anissa could go.

The pain in his chest was sharp. A woman next to him coughed loudly, giving him a disapproving stare as if he'd just done something terrible.

He took a deep breath and started pushing his way through the crowd towards the stairs. What had he said? What had he done?

He stopped and picked up the silver sandal lying on one side. His insides coiled. She'd been so anxious to get out of there she'd actually left a sandal behind.

He'd thought offering her the chance to move somewhere new and make a fresh start would be just what she needed—and just what she would want.

But he'd obviously got it wrong. Badly wrong.

Or maybe the thing he'd got wrong was that fact that he'd told her he loved her. He couldn't deny how he felt. But it was clear Anissa didn't feel the same way.

He reached the top of the stairs and stopped for a second as the hairs on the back of his neck prickled. Maybe she'd felt pressured by what he'd said. If Anissa didn't feel the same way, how must his declaration of love have felt?

Had he imagined the sparks and electricity between them—was he really that out of touch? He grabbed the banister to steady himself.

He'd been happy. He'd been caught up in the atmosphere of the night, the beauty of the woman in front of him and his own raw emotions.

He loved her. He loved her. He wanted her to be happy. He'd thought his offer of staying here and not worrying about training any more would have been a relief to her.

How wrong he'd been.

When she'd mentioned the other job he'd assumed she'd been considering it. She'd just been so much brighter and happier since they'd reached New York.

But it seemed she hadn't quite realised that yet.

He hurried out into the foyer and glanced from side to side, the elegant silver sandal in his hand. Surely she couldn't have gone anywhere without it?

The irony gripped him. He'd called her Ice Princess, but the truth was she was his Cinderella.

And she'd slipped right through his grasp.

# CHAPTER TEN

SHE'D PANICKED. SHE'D run straight out of the main entrance of the hotel into the snow-covered streets and flagged down the first taxi that she'd seen.

The cab driver had looked a little bewildered at the girl with one shoe, a silver purse hanging from her wrist, and a pile of skirts in her hands, but—being New York—he'd probably seen a whole lot more.

But when he'd asked her for an address her brain had frozen.

He gave a nod and started the cab, driving a few blocks and pulling over again. 'Okay, girl?' His question was quiet. There was concern on his face.

Her brain snapped back into focus. She knew what she must look like. He must be wondering if something had happened.

She nodded her head quickly. 'I'm sorry. I'm

okay.' He raised his eyebrows a little and she nodded again. 'I promise.'

The kindness of strangers. It brought a tear to her eye. She wondered what else this taxi driver had seen over the years. She rattled off the first address that sprang to mind. Jules. The only other person she knew in New York. She thought about pulling out her phone and checking to see if Jules was in. But the truth was, whether Jules was in or not, she'd no place else she felt she could go.

If Jules wasn't in she could always just wait outside.

The taxi driver gave a nod and pulled back out into the traffic.

The city that never slept. There was never a truer word. Even though it was after midnight, the streets of New York were still busy. Lots of people were laughing and joking in the streets—it was almost just as busy as it had been during the day.

She started to say a silent prayer that Jules hadn't gone out for the evening. What bar had they met in before? Maybe Anissa should try there. She glanced down at the ballgown and pulled a face. She might just be a little overdressed for a bar.

The taxi pulled up outside Jules's apartment and Anissa thanked the driver and jumped out, her bare foot instantly coming into contact with the freezing ground as she limped to the door-way.

She winced and pressed Jules's buzzer. 'Please be in, please be in,' she repeated, hoping against hope it might have some magical effect.

Thankfully, as soon as she'd sounded the buzzer Jules answered the door. Her eyes swept up and down Anissa's length before she stepped outside and slid her arm around Anissa, ushering her in.

Anissa was embarrassed. She'd allowed the hem of Jules's beautiful gown to be caught in the dirty snow on the streets of New York.

'I didn't know where to go,' she gasped. 'I'm sorry for turning up so late.'

Jules's face was set firmly. She hurried Anissa across her living room and settled her on the sofa before sitting on the low table in front of her.

'What happened?'

Anissa couldn't help herself. She started babbling. 'Oh, the dress. I'm sorry. I didn't mean to get it dirty. But I lost a shoe on my way out and couldn't go back for it. I'll pay for any repairs.'

She was suddenly conscious of the fact she was back in Jules's living room. All around her was the gorgeous array of glittering dresses on headless mannequins. She gave a little shiver as she pulled the firm bodice of her dress away from her skin.

She'd practically ruined one of these beautiful dresses. Jules would be mad. She would be right to be mad. Something else Anissa had messed up.

Tears started to fall down her face. 'I'm sorry, lots of people asked about the dress. I told them who designed it. I told everyone who spoke to me.'

Jules shook her head and frowned, leaning over and putting her warm hand over Anissa's cold one. 'Stop it. Stop talking about the dress.' She picked up the tablet sitting on the table and spun it around. 'I know you told everyone I'm the designer. You've already hit the news websites.'

Anissa let out a gasp and pulled the tablet towards her. There she was, standing on the red carpet with Leo's arm around her waist. They were looking at each other and smiling as though there wasn't anyone else around them. As if they were actually in a private bubble all of their own.

They looked like a golden couple. And in Jules's stunning dress she looked like a princess.

Jules pointed to the headline: *'Billionaire's Date is Belle of the Ball'*.

She spoke carefully. 'You've done me a million favours by wearing my dress. But push that aside. What's wrong, Anissa? What happened tonight? Are you hurt?'

Anissa's throat was tight. Hot tears spilled down her cheeks and her whole body tensed. 'No. No. No one hurt me.'

Jules watched her for a few seconds, eyeing her carefully before giving a little nod of acceptance. 'Okay, so you're not hurt. So why have you turned up here...' she looked down at the floor '...in the middle of the night and missing a shoe?' Jules gave her head a little shake. 'What did Mr Wonderful do?'

Anissa had finally started to breathe again. Her head was beginning to clear. She was here. She was in Jules's house. She could stop. She could think.

'He told me he loved me and asked me to stay.' The words just burst from her mouth and she dissolved into tears again. This time it wasn't just a few tears streaming down her cheeks. This time it was all out sobbing.

After a few quiet seconds Jules moved from the table and sat on the sofa next to Anissa, putting her arm around her and letting her rest her head on Jules's shoulder while she sobbed.

It was almost as if everything that had been bubbling under the surface for so long had finally erupted. All the pent-up frustrations about who she was, what she was doing, and whether she'd be good enough again flowed from her. Her feelings for Leo had just brought everything to the surface. After years of being driven by an ambitious ex, she'd finally met someone who loved her for who she was—not who she could be.

After a while Jules patted her back. When she spoke her voice had an amused tone. 'Anissa, I'm trying to work out why it's such a disaster that a gorgeous billionaire has told you that he loves you, and asked you to stay in New York?'

'Don't say it like that,' Anissa pleaded, knowing exactly how ironic it sounded.

'How would you like me to say it?' asked Jules.

Anissa's phone buzzed again. It had buzzed almost continuously on the journey over here. She didn't even have to turn it over to know who it was.

She shook her head fiercely. 'I can't. I just can't. He told me that the gold medal was probably out of my reach. He told me to consider other plans. He wanted me to have a back-up plan. I'm not ready.'

Jules pulled back a little and gave her a look that was way beyond her young years.

'That's it,' she said succinctly.

Anissa wiped some tears away. 'What's it?'

Jules gave a nod of her head. 'That's what the issue is, Anissa. And now you have to ask yourself why.'

Anissa was thoroughly confused. 'What do you mean?'

Jules pushed herself up and walked through to the kitchen and switched on the coffee pot. She turned to face Anissa. 'You said you're not ready. That's the crux of the matter. Now, you have to ask yourself why. *Why* are you not ready? He hasn't said anything to you that you haven't already considered yourself.'

Anissa shivered, even though the room was warm. She wasn't sure she liked this line of questioning.

'Do you love him?' The question seemed to come out of the blue.

'I... I... I...' Anissa stumbled over the words.

Jules raised her eyebrows and walked back from the kitchen with a mug in either hand.

'Do you love him?' This time she was much firmer.

This time she didn't think, the answer just bubbled over. 'Of course I love him.'

There it was. How she felt. How she'd been feeling these last few days. She'd finally admitted it—she'd finally said it out loud.

Now it was real.

Jules eyebrows were still raised. 'And that,' she said as she waved the cups in the air, 'is why we need coffee.'

Four cups of coffee later the early morning light was streaming into the room. Jules was lying on the sofa, her eyelids heavy. But Anissa hadn't slept at all. She'd switched to hot water with lemon but every part of her body was still jangling.

The pale blue dress was now back on one of the mannequins. The bottom edges looked as if they had been dragged through a muddy puddle, and even from across the room Anissa could see that some of the sequins were hanging off.

She'd changed into a T-shirt and jeans belonging to Jules, along with a pair of thick socks and baseball boots.

Jules gave a groan and snuggled into one of the cushions on the sofa. She was obviously all talked out.

Even though Anissa had been drinking for hours, her throat still felt dry. Leo had told her that he loved her and she'd run away. He'd asked her to live with him and she'd practically bolted.

Instead of focusing on the fact she'd met a

good, kind-hearted man who made her heart swell, she'd focused on her past. She'd focused on failure.

Her breathing stuttered and, as if in sympathy for Leo, the muscles in her legs and back ached.

The chronic, persistent and sometimes unbearable ache she felt after skiing. The thing she'd ignored before her accident, and even more so after.

Her body telling her that she'd never reach the gold medal. Not now, not after she'd done so much damage. The truth was, even if she spent the next five years practising every day, she still wouldn't be able to match her previous skill and speed.

Her body had been telling her for a while—her brain just hadn't been listening.

'I'm never going to get a gold medal,' she breathed as she stared at the ice-cold New York street outside.

'What?' Jules rubbed her eyes. 'What did you say?'

'I'm never going to get a gold medal.' This time her words were more assured. 'I'm never going to be good enough to compete. I'm never going to reach the speed I need.'

It was the oddest sensation. Like self-discovery. Her brain had finally put the pieces together. But saying them out loud was like an affirmation. A confirmation to herself that this was real. She swayed, her legs instantly feeling like jelly. She bent down and put her head in her hands.

Within a few seconds she realised Jules had rolled herself off the sofa and come over next to her. Jules's warm hand closed over her own as they clutched her head. Her hair was still on top of her head. She couldn't even imagine what it looked like at this stage.

'I've been a fool,' she whispered as she lifted her head to meet Jules's weary gaze. 'I've been such a fool.'

Jules sighed and collapsed on the floor next to her. 'Okay, I'm too tired. And my phone has been buzzing all night. You're going to have to spell it out for me.'

Anissa nodded. Then stopped and shook her head instead. 'My head has been full of skiing and winning the championship for so long, it's like I just couldn't imagine anything else.' She brushed away one of the tears in her eyes. 'Leo brought me here to show me another world. He knew. He knew I'd probably never get back to professional skiing, but he was trying to tell me that there's so much more out there. He wanted me to see a whole other world.' She sat back on her heels. 'But I just wasn't listening,' she said sadly.

Jules screwed up her face. 'But your heart was listening. You told me that you loved him. Surely that's all you need to know.'

Anissa sat up straighter, her hands going automatically to her heart. The panic that had gripped her last night was starting again in a weird, different kind of way.

'I have to find Leo,' she said, pushing herself to her feet.

Jules squinted up at her. 'What?'

Anissa reached for her purse. 'I have to get back. I have to get back to Leo. I didn't tell him. I didn't even tell him that I love him too. What if he thinks I don't?'

Jules gave a smile. 'Does this mean I can finally get some sleep?'

Anissa reached over and gave her a huge hug. 'Jules, you're wonderful. You can definitely get some sleep. And you are the most fabulous, talented dress designer on the entire planet. Thank you for helping me out.'

Jules shook her head and stood up, dragging herself over to the sofa and flopping back down. 'Go.' She waved her arm.

'Go and tell your billionaire that you've finally worked things out and that you love him.'

She laughed as she closed her eyes and pulled the cushion over her head. 'Please, do it now.'

Anissa nodded and headed straight to the door. She could phone. He'd texted her for the first few hours after she'd left. But the phone didn't seem right. Not for now. Not for this.

She stepped out into the cold morning air. She had no jacket. She'd forgotten to ask Jules for a coat and the biting wind chilled her to the bone.

She waved her hand wildly, trying to flag down a cab. After a few minutes one appeared with its light on and slowed down. She climbed in and quickly recited Leo's address, settling back in the seat and praying her heart would stop thudding by the time she reached there.

New York had never looked so grey. Leo had finally stopped texting Anissa and just prayed she was safe. He hadn't slept a wink. He was still wearing last night's tux. Maybe she'd booked into some random hotel rather than come back here. Or maybe she'd jumped on a plane back to Mont Coeur—anything rather than see him again.

There was a click behind him and he spun around. Anissa stepped out of the penthouse elevator, her cheeks flushed pink. Her hair was still piled on her head in a lopsided kind of way.

He could see remnants of last night's glitter on her cheeks, but she'd completely changed her clothes. She was wearing a rumpled T-shirt, jeans and baseball shoes and she was rubbing her arms frantically.

He couldn't stop himself. 'Where have you been?'

She stepped forward. 'I'm sorry. I'm sorry. I just didn't know... You took me unawares... I wasn't expecting... I mean... I just...' She couldn't seem to get the words out.

All he could feel was relief that she was actually here. Actually back in his apartment. After last night, he'd wondered if he'd ever see her again. And the thought of that, of never actually seeing Anissa again, had made him feel physically sick.

'Take a minute, Anissa.'

He wanted to reach over and put his arms around her. But he wasn't sure what she wanted. She might just be here to pick up her things and leave again, and that just tore his heart apart.

She stepped up right in front of him. She was trembling. Was it because she was cold or was it because of something else? All he could see was her wide pale blue eyes. Her skin was almost translucent.

Her cold hands reached out towards him. Her

touch sent a pulse of electricity up his arm. But he still didn't want to move. He'd already got things so wrong. He didn't want to presume anything.

'You brought me here,' she started. She gestured to the world through the windows behind him. 'You brought me here to show me another world. One I'd never experienced before. I'd been so focused on skiing. It was everything.' She clutched her hands to her chest. 'My life. My passion. My heart. I couldn't think outside the skiing box. Not even when I was injured. Not even when I should have taken a step back to reassess.'

He was holding his breath. He wanted to hear what came next.

'You've shown me a whole other world, Leo. One with possibilities. The chance to work on the skiing committee is a big one. And if I'd still been in Mont Coeur, training every day, I would never have considered it—not for a second.'

She gave her head a shake and smiled a sad smile. 'I was so focused on winning a gold medal. I thought it was the only dream to have, the only goal to dream about. I couldn't see past that. And because I couldn't see past that, I've missed a whole life. I've missed a whole world.'

She pressed her lips together and met his gaze. 'You showed me something else, Leo. You showed me that someone can love me for being me. Not for being a potential gold-medal winner.' She pulled one of her hands back and put it on her heart. 'I've never had that before. I've never experienced it, and I didn't know it was possible.' She took a deep breath. 'I've never thought I was good enough.'

He opened his mouth to speak but hesitated when she shook her head. She gave a soft smile. 'I'm so sorry, Leo. I've been having doubts about myself for the last year. Something I didn't want to admit to, and was trying to totally ignore. I was taking painkillers constantly to try and deal with the agony I'd be in after training hard. I'd begun to accept it as normal, rather than take a deep breath and ask myself if it was right for me. Getting away from Mont Coeur and actually having a holiday was completely new for me.' She reached out to him again.

'And I know you've had so much going on. I understand how hard everything has been for you. Every day I've spent with you, I've realised just how much you mean to me. It doesn't matter that it's only been a few weeks. I've managed to get to twenty-eight years old without feeling like this. It scared me, Leo. It scared me. I'm sorry. I'm sorry I ran out last night.'

Now he wanted to breathe. Now he actually wanted to hope.

She touched his cheek as tears filled her eyes and her voice shook. 'I love you, Leo Baxter. I've never met anyone like you. You have the biggest heart in the world, and I want you to share it with me. I want you to share it with your family. I want you to know how lucky they are to have you. I want you to know that your parents would be proud of the man you've become. They couldn't have possibly hoped for any better.'

If he held his breath any longer he might fall over. This time he wasn't scared to reach out and touch her.

'When you ran away last night I thought I'd got everything wrong. I thought I'd imagined the connection we had. I thought I'd scared you off.'

She stepped closer and ran her fingers through his hair. 'You didn't imagine the connection, Leo. It's been there from the first second. I just couldn't let myself acknowledge it. I thought I only had room in my life for skiing, for reaching for that gold medal. I was wrong, Leo. I've never loved anyone before like this—that's why it's so scary.'

He chose his words carefully. 'Anissa, you can be anything you want to be. If you still want to pursue your dream of skiing, I'll support you completely.' And it was true. He'd be there for her whatever she decided to do.

She shook her head as she pressed her lips together for a second. 'I needed to get here, Leo. I needed to get to this place myself. I needed to realise what I was doing to my body and that I wasn't being realistic with my dreams.'

She couldn't hide more tears as she blinked. 'I can't pretend it hasn't been hard.'

He understood that. He knew that. But she gave another smile. 'You've helped me, more than you could ever know. Thanks to you I know there's something else out there.' She shook her head. 'I don't want to pursue my dream of skiing. But I would like to take up the offer from the Championship Skiing Committee. I'd like a chance to encourage others to realise their dreams.'

The excitement was in her eyes. He could see she'd actually found something to be passionate about.

'That sounds perfect.' He spoke cautiously, wondering what that meant for them.

She nodded slowly. 'But I only want to do it if we can be together. I don't want to be at the other side of the world from you. I love you,

Leo. I want to be with you. If I take that job it will mean lots of travel, all over the US and overseas. But the truth is I don't really want us to be apart.'

His heart swelled in his chest. It was just what he wanted to hear. He pulled her towards him and put his lips on hers. She returned his kisses passionately, wrapping her arms around his neck. 'It's just as well, then, that I own a private jet and can take you, and follow you, to the ends of the earth. When you need to go overseas, I can come with you—if you want me to—and work from there. When you're in the US, we can base ourselves here, in New York. We can make this work, Anissa. I know we can.'

'I thought I'd been a fool,' she whispered. 'I thought I'd lost you.'

'Ditto,' he whispered, then he pulled back a little and laughed. Having Anissa back in his arms felt so right.

It was almost as if his head had finally started to clear. Realising he loved Anissa was just the starting point. 'I might have done something that would surprise you last night.'

She tilted her head to one side. 'What?'

'I phoned Sebastian again.' He stopped for a second and tried the words again. 'I phoned my brother.'

She pulled back, her eyes wide. 'You did?'

He nodded. 'I did.'

'What on earth did you say to him?'

'I told him I'd brought the woman I loved to New York and I'd messed up. I told him that I'd asked her stay with me and she'd run away.'

'What did he say?' Anissa asked cautiously.

Leo gave an amused nod. 'I think it took him a few moments to get over the shock that I'd called—and that I'd told him all that.'

'And then?'

'And then he told me to take a deep breath. He said if I loved you, I had to give you space. I had to respect your decision. He said I should wait and let you come back to me—if you wanted to.'

Anissa looked a little surprised. 'He didn't tell you try a big gesture, or to hunt the city for me?'

Leo shook his head. 'No. Because that's exactly what I wanted to do. He told me I'd made the big gesture and I had to let love decide what happened next.'

She slid her arms around his waist. 'Wow. From a guy who hated you to a brother who gives advice.'

Leo nodded slowly as he looked out over New York. He sighed. 'I love this place. But

I need to get to know Sebastian and Noemi. I don't want to be part of the jewellery business, but I need to find my place in my family. It scares me, Anissa. It scares me more than you can know.'

She gave his waist a squeeze. 'But I do get it, Leo. More than you can understand. I had to make a decision. I had to be brave. Twice. I had to decide to walk away from the only career I had known. And I had to decide to give my heart to someone.' She stood on tiptoe and whispered in his ear, 'And once you do it… it's not that hard. The thought is actually a lot scarier than the process.' She winked at him. 'And you've already done one.'

A slow smile came over him as a warm sensation swept over his body. She was right. He knew she was right. Exposing his heart to Anissa had been his first step. The first step to forming real relationships in his life. Maybe, with her help, he could take the next step.

He pulled her backwards with him and sat in one of the big chairs, pulling her onto his lap. 'The beauty of a private jet means that you can more or less go anywhere you want, anytime. So, if I asked the woman I love to come with me—to come back with me to Mont Coeur to meet my family—what would she say?'

Anissa wound her hands back around his neck as she settled in his lap. Her eyes were shining brightly. 'I would say try and stop me.'

And then she kissed him and made him forget about everything else.

\* \* \* \* \*

*Welcome to*
*The Cattaneos' Christmas Miracles trilogy*

*If you enjoyed this story,*
*look out for the next two books*

**Heiress's Royal Baby Bombshell**
*by Jennifer Faye*
**CEO's Marriage Miracle**
*by Sophie Pembroke*

*Coming soon!*